CHRISTOPHER

CHRISTOPHER

Richard M. Koff

Illustrations by Barbara Reinertson

A Dawne-Leigh Book

Celestial Arts
Millbrae, California

Copyright © 1981 by Richard M. Koff

Illustrations Copyright © 1981 by Barbara Reinertson

Celestial Arts
231 Adrian Road
Millbrae, CA 94030

First Printing, September, 1981
Manufactured in the United States of America

Library of Congress in Publication Data

Koff, Richard M.
     Christopher.

     "A Dawne-Leigh book."
     Summary: Thirteen-year-old Christopher enters a
supposedly haunted house on a dare where he meets a
mysterious man who teaches him to use mental powers
he never knew existed.
     [1. Occult sciences—Fiction] I. Reinertson,
Barbara, ill.   II. Title.
PZ7.K8193Ch   [Fic]   81-65885
ISBN 0-89742-050-0   AACR2

To my two Christophers
who are both in this book,
and in this character.

Contents

Christopher could feel the sharp edges of the brick schoolyard wall cutting into his shoulders. They had backed him into it, taunting and sneering just because he bragged a little about the old house on Sheridan Road.

"I have too been in it. Lots of times," he shouted over their jeers.

Skinny as an ice cream stick, he was no match for Johnny Dawes or Sam who were both older, taller, and heavier than he. But Christopher knew that they would back down if he let his temper loose. For a second he felt like hauling off and swinging at them, but his mother would have a fit if he got into another fight. Instead he said, "All right. I'll prove it—if you guys will come with me."

"Sure you will," Johnny said with heavy sarcasm. "Do we have to ring the doorbell and open the door for you, too?"

"Nope. If you're scared you can watch from across the street." He could feel the wildness rising inside him as it did whenever he was pushed into something. Briefly he wondered why he had started the argument, but now he could barely breathe, his chest was so tight. He pushed his way past them and headed over toward Sheridan Road.

[1]

It was a big, gloomy castle of a house sitting in the middle of an otherwise pleasant street. Johnny and Sam were following at a safe distance. They were so quiet that Christopher turned quickly to see if they were still there. When he saw their faces he decided they were probably more scared than he was.

He turned between the tall weeds and walked up the steps. It was dim and damp under the porch roof. To the left of the front door a rusty chain hung with a rough wooden handle. He pulled it down and when he let go he heard a faint tinkle from inside.

The door opened slowly, but quietly, and a man stood looking at him with a small smile.

"You must be Christopher," he said.

"Ummm. Yes, sir," he said. The man was small, not much taller than Christopher, and very thin. Everything about him was skinny. He had long thin fingers, his shoulders were narrow and hunched together. His eyes were deep in their sockets and shadowed.

"Come in," he said and led the way. Christopher took one last look at his friends, but they had already gone. In fact the street looked different—darker and misted.

He went in and the door closed behind him with an ominous click. Inside, it was unexpectedly bright and cheerful. The man climbed up onto the seat of an old wooden organ at one side of the front hall. He put his feet on the pedals carefully and said, "I just want to finish this. I'll be with you in a minute."

Then he started to play. At first it was so quiet that Christopher could barely hear the thin, reedy melody. Then it came closer and louder, and other sounds joined in the melody until it filled the room and seemed to be sounding right inside Christopher's head. It was faster and faster, spinning him around and around. He held his arms out wide like a helicopter or a windmill and let it take him faster and faster. His head seemed lighter as he spun and soon it almost lifted right off his shoulders. He closed his eyes and kept going around and around with the music, faster and faster, until he felt himself sliding, sliding away. . . .

[2]

Christopher awoke to the smell of fresh-cut grass in his nose. It was the man's breath near his face. He was lying on a leather couch in a room filled with books. A great carved wooden desk stood in front of a window. Christopher touched the cool cloth the man was holding to his head.

"You're not afraid now, are you?" He smiled down at Christopher. "I like that about you." He went behind the desk. "You'll be all right. Get up when you feel like it."

Christopher sat up carefully, aware of a dizziness still, but otherwise feeling okay. The man had opened one of the lower drawers of the desk and pulled out a pale blue folder.

"Yes, this is it. Christopher Cove, right?" He looked up as Christopher nodded. "Hmmm. Thirteen years old. Four feet, ten inches, 102 pounds." He looked up again. "That's about right."

Christopher shrugged. He had no idea how much he weighed.

"Father a lawyer, mother in advertising. Not much time for you, huh?"

Christopher didn't bother to answer that one. He had plenty of time with his parents when he wanted it. They were so boring most of the time.

"Been in the house on Forest Avenue for three years now. Came from St. Louis before that. You like it better here?"

Christopher said, "Yes, sir." He decided to try good-kid-Wenceslaus on the man, who didn't seem to notice.

"IQ 187, PQ 154, SQ 210." He stared at Christopher in a speculative way. "That's pretty good. 'Definitely a possibility,' as one of your philosophers might say." He took a last look at a note at the bottom of the page. "Oh, yes. There's that, too. Well, we'll just have to work on it, won't we?"

He closed the folder with a slap, tucked it back into the drawer and then leaned his chin on his clasped hands. For a full minute they just sat there looking at each other. The silence built a tension in Christopher that made him distinctly uncomfortable. Finally, unable to resist, he said, "What's a PQ, sir? And an SQ?"

"SQ is sensitivity—intuition, nonverbal stuff, picking up signals through your eyes and other senses rather than by rational understanding. PQ is—well, I'll have to explain that some other day. You obviously need some training and exercise there."

"Yes, sir." Christopher said. "Uhh. You have a very beautiful home here, sir."

"Home? This isn't my home, son. This is my office."

Christopher hated to be called "son" by anyone, including his father. An office? Maybe he was a writer or something.

"I can see you're confused. Let's get a few things straight right at the start here. I am a teacher, not a writer, or a lawyer like your father. This is my schoolroom. The rest of the building is for files, offices, and experimental laboratories, which we'll be working in from time to time."

"Yes, sir." Christopher was always careful in the presence of crazy people since you never knew which way they would jump. It was clear this man had lost most of his marbles.

"You are my newest student," the man went on.

Christopher threw his eyes up to the ceiling. What he really didn't need was another adult teaching him things that were going to be "good for him." He moved forward to the edge of the couch, ready to go.

"Yes, it's almost time for the bell," the man said. "Your first lesson is over and as soon as I give you your homework assignment you can leave."

Homework? This was really too much. As it was, Christopher never did the assignments Miss Rooney gave him at school.

The man stood, and then went over to a chest that was built into the bookshelves. Inside were many narrow drawers padded with black velvet. The man drew out one drawer and Christopher could see that it was filled with small cubes of gold, each in its own little padded compartment. The man took one out and examined it closely.

[4]

"No, this is number 101. We want 001." He tapped his fingers over one drawer. "Yes. Here we are." He selected a cube and pushed the drawer back. He went back to the desk and sat down. He took the blue folder out of the drawer again, made a penciled entry on a form, and slipped it back into the drawer.

"My name is Fentonborough Plateau, near as you can say it, but you may call me 'Headmaster,' and I suggest you get into the habit of thinking about me that way. I shall call you Christopher. We will have a number of lessons like this one. In a while the course will be completed. There is no final examination in this school. If you have passed, you will know it. If not, you won't remember very much about it at all.

"You will come here for lessons from time to time. You are not to discuss the lessons with anyone. You had better be very clear about that. Not with anyone, do you understand? Not with your mother or father, friends, or other teachers. No one."

He waited for a response so Christopher nodded, humoring him.

He sighed. "They wouldn't believe you anyway, and you might get into trouble."

He closed his eyes briefly as if to consult a checklist written on the back of his lids. "The homework assignments are each in a talisman like this one." He held up his hand. "Do you know binary numbers?"

Christopher nodded, a little uncertainly.

"A nod is not an answer." There was a whip-snap in his voice.

"Yes, umm, Headmaster. I think so, sir." He had heard of binary numbers in math class and knew they had to do with computers, but that was all. Mostly he just wanted to get out of there.

"No matter. You'll figure them out quickly enough. This is number 001, which corresponds to your number one." He took the gold cube and held it between his thumb and middle finger.

"You squeeze the talisman just before you are ready to start your homework."

[5]

He smiled again at the look in Christopher's eyes. "Don't worry, it won't hurt you."

Just then a chime sounded from somewhere deep in the house. "There's the bell. First lesson is over. Off with you now. Don't forget the assignment."

Christopher took the gold cube. It was warm and unexpectedly heavy.

"But what am I supposed to do?" he asked.

"Oh, you'll know." He threw his head back and barked a loud laugh to the ceiling. "You'll know." He led Christopher quickly to the front door and held it open.

Christopher ran down the street and over to his own block. His mother would be phoning from her office to check up on him, and anyway he was hungry for dinner. He felt the "homework talisman" in his pocket. He liked the look of the little cube. It felt smooth and precious.

Crackers started barking frantically and scratching at the kitchen door as Christopher climbed the back porch stairs of his house. Crackers was a big, gangly Irish setter, all floppy ears and liquid motion. His paws and tail seemed to be loosely connected to his legs and body, so he looked like a big rag doll as he jumped up and licked at Christopher's face.

"Okay, Crackers. Okay. Take it easy." Christopher hugged him close so that the tongue wouldn't get all over his face, and then scratched his stomach and tickled it a bit so Crackers fell back with that silly grin he sometimes got.

"Where you been?" Frances asked in exasperation. "I wanted to leave early tonight. Your ma's been on the phone twice already and your dinner's burnt to a crisp. I'm going to turn it off and you go wash and call your ma. No," as he started up the back stairs, "you'd better call her first, then wash. I'm late so I'm leaving right now. You put the dishes in the washer when you're through, hear?" And without giving him time to say a word, she gathered up her purse and shopping bag and stomped out the front door.

Christopher went into the kitchen with Crackers rubbing against his leg. A dried-up, sad excuse for a hamburger lay greasy in the center of a small frying pan on the stove. The buns were in a plastic wrapper alongside. He lifted the cooling hamburger with his fingers and smelled it. Then he just dropped his hand casually to his side and Crackers took the meat eagerly. He carried it over to his dish in the corner of the kitchen and gulped it down.

The only good thing Frances had left was a paper napkin full of french fries. Christopher grabbed a handful and started nibbling as he slumped at the kitchen table with a glass of grape juice, making a purple moustache on his upper lip. He needed to think a minute before calling his mother.

He sighed. Parents were such a pain. He finished off the last of the french fries and washed them down with grape juice. His fingers were a little greasy so the telephone nearly slipped out of his hand as he picked it up to dial her office number. The secretary had already gone so his mother answered it herself.

"Hi, Mom. Frances just left. I had a flat tire on the bike up on Lake Street and had to walk all the way home. When are you coming home? Could we have pizza tonight?" He didn't want to give her too much time to pick his story apart.

"Wait a minute. Not so fast. You could have called, you know. And I'm not paying for any new bicycle tubes this time. Didn't Frances get dinner for you?"

"Just a crummy hamburger. You know she can't cook them the way you do. Why can't we have pizza? I'm still hungry."

"Absolutely not. You had one last night. I think that's why you keep having those stomachaches. Make yourself another hamburger if you like, or a peanut butter sandwich.

"Now listen to me, young man. You're supposed to call when you're going to be late. Frances worried and so did I. She wanted to leave by five, and it doesn't seem too much to ask that a thirteen-year-old have some consideration for others once in a while."

[8]

He could hear her getting up steam again. "No. You may not have a pizza tonight." If that was the extent of his punishment he was nicely off the hook.

"Your father and I have to stay downtown for dinner tonight and we may not be home until after ten. Your sister, Penny, will probably be late too. Don't bother asking, Bill can't come over when we aren't there. Anyway it's a school night. I don't want any mess or any fights with Penny."

She could get ahead of him sometimes, and he was really frustrated when that happened because he had no outlet for the ideas that buzzed in his head all the time.

"And don't go out again. It's dark and I want you home. I'll be calling again later from the restaurant. Be good, Christopher, and we'll see you before you go to sleep."

She hung up before he had a chance to try for the pizza again, since they were going to be out for the evening. He looked at the dirty pan. His stomach was growling. There had to be something in the pantry. He opened the refrigerator door and stood looking at the shelves full of things like fruit, vegetables, leftovers. They never seemed to have anything worth eating. Leaving the door open he went to the shelves of the pantry. There was a do-it-yourself pizza package and he decided to make one.

By the time he got it into the oven there was flour dusted all over the kitchen and tomato sauce on the floor. He would have time to take a shower while the pizza was cooking, but before going upstairs he called Bill, who lived in the next block, to tell him not to call until later because he was going to take a shower.

"Did you go to the old house?" Bill would have heard from Johnny Dawes.

"Yeah."

"What was it like? Who lives there?" None of them had ever seen anyone come or go from the old house and they all thought only ghosts lived there now.

"The door was unlocked when I got there so I just went in. It's all cobwebs and spiders. There are old newspapers all over the floor and the place smells like there's something—or someone—dead upstairs. I couldn't stay long because the rats were biting at my shoes and the ghost of the dead old lady started screaming at me."

"Aw, go on. You're just putting me on." Bill wasn't really sure, but he didn't want to appear too gullible.

"You don't have to believe me, but you can come with me the next time I go and see for yourself."

"You going back?" Bill's voice began to squeak a little. "When?"

"Oh, I don't know. When the old ghost lady invites me to tea, I guess."

A little of the sauce had dripped to the bottom of the oven and began to burn and smoke. "Gotta go, Bill. Talk to you later," and he hung up.

He took a little wine from the decanter on the sideboard, but it tasted sour so he settled for a mixture of cola and the last of the grape juice. He carried the pizza pan and the glass up to his room and set it on the little table in front of the television. Crackers came up and sniffed at the hot pizza, but Christopher shooed him away and turned on the set. They settled down together on one of the large beanbags and watched happily while he munched on the pizza.

Later he went downstairs to get some ice cream and a few brownies from the jar. When he wandered into the living room some ice cream dripped on the rug, so he rubbed it carefully with his bare foot. He sat at the desk his father used in the corner of the living room. There were drawing paper and pads in the bottom drawer, he knew. He put the ice cream dish on the corner of the desk and poked through the drawer. Some of the papers fell on the floor when he pulled out a sheet of red drawing paper. He tried the black marking pen on it. The color soaked through the red to his father's papers on the desk and left a horrible purplish color.

He finished his ice cream while idly pushing through the mail stacked on the desk, but when he saw he was leaving ice cream smears he decided he had better go to take his shower after all.

As usual Frances had left his bathroom impossibly neat. He looked in the mirror. His face was smeared with chocolate ice cream and grape juice. He opened his mouth and looked at his tongue. It was purple, too. He took the toothbrush and then had the usual search for the toothpaste, which Frances insisted on putting in the medicine cabinet where he always looked for it last.

He brushed his teeth, leaving the toothpaste open on the sink where he'd be able to find it in the morning, and then stripped off his clothes, letting them fall where they were. He went out to the linen closet to get one of the big bath towels. For some reason Frances insisted on leaving him only little ones in his bathroom and kept the big ones for his parents. They never used them anyway.

Then, remembering that Penny might be coming home any time now, he rushed back to his room and carefully closed the door. He started the water for the shower. It always took forever for the water to get hot, so he sat on the floor of the bathroom with the towel over his knees and looked at the pipes under the sink. That Headmaster was not too bad a guy, he thought. He remembered the spinning, flying sensation as the music rose around him and he thought he might like to hear that again, only this time sitting down so he wouldn't get so dizzy.

He reached around to his jeans and dug out the little gold cube. The bathroom was steamy from the hot shower now, but he wanted to look at it before getting in. He turned it so that he could see the engraving. It had two zeros and a numeral one etched in its front face. As he held it, it seemed to get warm and glow faintly. He pressed gently on either side with his thumb and middle finger.

Nothing happened, so he squeezed a little harder. Still nothing. He shrugged and set the cube carefully on the side of the bathtub. He prepared to face the music and get under the shower. He'd need shampoo. Frances always put the shampoo up on the windowsill. He reached for it and noticed the back of his hand. There were dozens of tiny black dots on it. At first he thought it was just sprinkled dirt, but they were all perfectly round and equally spaced on his hand, as if printed. He looked at the other hand. Sure enough he had them there as well. If anything they looked bigger. He held them under the sink faucet and ran some water on them. The dots didn't wash off. Even with soap they didn't want to wash off. Instead, they seemed to be spreading and getting bigger as he scrubbed.

In fact they were now definitely getting bigger and moving up his wrists and arms, and even changing color a little! They were now purple and blue and a dark green and even red! He started to rub at them with soap and the brush, scrubbing as hard as he could. But it didn't seem to have any effect. They were getting worse. Now there was no doubt that they were all different colors: red and yellow, blue and purple, green, orange, and white. They grew and spread up his arms and across his chest looking for all the world like clown paint. When he looked in the mirror he could see a white one on his cheek and a red one on his forehead and up under his hair.

He ran the hottest water he could stand and scrubbed and scraped at his hands, but the soapy lather didn't have the slightest effect on the dots! What was happening to him? He wondered if he had caught some awful disease and for a minute imagined himself lying in a coffin all covered in polka dots, while his mother wept and his father looked sad. It would serve them right, he thought, for all the times they could have kissed him instead of spanking him.

But he didn't want to die. He opened his mouth wide and looked at his tongue. They were there, in his mouth, too! And now his hair was beginning to change color in round areas. Quickly he swept the shower curtain aside and hopped into the tub. The water cascaded down over his head splashing on the floor. He grabbed the shampoo from the windowsill and upturned the bottle over his wet head. He scrubbed and scrubbed up a thick lather and then rubbed it down over his face and across his chest. Then he sluiced off the soap, scattering spray and lather in all directions. He peeked carefully through squeezed-shut eyes at his stomach, but the dots were still there. He jumped out of the tub and held the towel to his wet head, but as he dried his face he saw that the dots were now on the bathtub and the tiles that lined the back wall. Small dots and big ones, every color of the rainbow, were spread all over the walls of the bathroom, on the towel in his hands, on the floor, across the mirror of the medicine cabinet, and on the back of the closed bathroom door.

Just then the door moved slowly aside. For a second he felt real panic, but then he saw Crackers' wet nose coming around the edge of the door. Crackers blinked as he looked into the room.

"Stay out, Crackers!" he shouted, but it was too late. He saw dots changing the beautiful rust red of Crackers' coat to a flat white and green and blue. Crackers spun around and started chewing his hair. Then he began to run frantically through the rooms with Christopher chasing after him, trying to keep him from spreading the awful dots throughout the rest of the house.

But he was too late, and with helpless horror he saw the dots slide up the living room walls and down over his mother's new beige couch. It was horrible. He stood in the middle of the living room rug, the big white towel still clutched around his waist, water dripping from his wet head, and he could feel the tears starting up behind his eyes.

He had been in lots of trouble in his life, he knew, but nothing ever compared to what he was going to get when his mother and father saw their house. Walls, rugs, furniture, even the lamp bulbs were covered with polka dots of every color. The windows had great dots glowing against the darkness of the night outside. Crackers whimpered and mooched up to him from behind the polka dot drapes where he had been hiding.

Christopher just sort of crumpled right there on the living room rug. The tears came pouring out and dripped tiny purple dots on the large circles of red and white that covered his palms. It just wasn't

[13]

fair, he thought. He buried his face in the towel. He couldn't stand
to look at the room anymore. It was warm under the towel and he
could smell the wetness of his body and Crackers' damp hair as he
snuggled up against him, his eyes closed too. He held him very tight

and buried his face in the hair. With his eyes closed it didn't seem quite so horrible. Maybe he could persuade his mother that polka dots looked wonderful in the living room. Better yet, wouldn't this be the perfect way to decorate for a Halloween party? It didn't really matter that Halloween was still four months off. Or wait a minute. What about the costume party his father was always teasing his mother about? He could say he decorated the house just for the occasion.

He giggled when he thought of the front door opening and the dots all getting out. They'd slide down the front steps and out onto the sidewalk. They'd go across the grass and up the trees and over the cars as they passed in the street.

Maybe they were outside already! He went to the front door and opened it just a crack. There were no dots on the front porch and he couldn't see any out on the sidewalk either.

He closed the door and ran back up to his room. He could see out of the windows into the backyard, but there were no dots out there. They were strictly in his house and he was going to be blamed. He went back to the bathroom and picked up the gold talisman. That Headmaster was a devil. Do you suppose his homework was to scrub off every polka dot in the house? There had to be millions of them!

Just then he heard the telltale screech of the garage door sliding open. His parents were home! Quickly he ran into his room, snapped off the light, and dove under the covers.

He closed his eyes tight and let go.

He didn't know any other way to describe the feeling. It was as if he took the hardest swing he could at some mean kid. It was as if he jumped off the top of the schoolyard fence. It was using all the power of his wiry body in one great earth-shattering shout. It was like blasting the enemy spaceship right out of existence with the concentrated beam of his anger.

He could feel something break loose inside his head and spill out all the trapped frustration that had collected there ever since he

[15]

could remember. And with the release came a relief, a relaxation. He held his eyes tightly shut and started to breathe slowly and deeply, as if fast asleep. He followed his parents in his imagination as they left the car (he heard the doors thunk shut), and then struggle with the back door which always stuck in warm weather. He heard them move into the kitchen and then, after a pause, walk quickly through the first floor. Then heavy steps came marching up the back stairs. He squeezed his eyes shut as tight as they could get and breathed deeply and slowly through his mouth.

"Christopher!" His mother was furious. She came stomping into his room and snapped on the light. "Can't you be left alone in this house for two hours without turning it into a shambles? Just look at this room, the kitchen, even the living room. What were you doing in the living room?"

It was no use. He sat up and faced her, the tears streaming down his cheeks, his eyes tightly shut.

"It's incredible!" She had that tight, nasty rasp in her voice that he really hated. "Burnt pizza all over the oven, which you might have thought to turn off. Ice cream all over the kitchen floor, and grape juice stains on the back stair rug. A filthy wet towel in the middle of the living room. Your father will take a strap to you once he gets his desk papers straightened out. What's the matter with you? Don't you have the slightest regard for other people's belongings?" She put her hand on his wet head.

"Look at me. What have you got to say for yourself? You can just get up and come downstairs. You're not going to bed or watching television or anything until you have put this house back the way you found it."

Carefully he opened his eyes. The scolding was the usual. Somehow it didn't seem as bad as he expected. He looked around.

"Mark my words, there'll be punishment this time. You're grounded for the rest of the week, and you can expect a spanking from your father as well. You hear me?"

He nodded, dazed, and looked around. He couldn't believe it. The dots were all gone! He seemed to have an after-image of them in his eyes as if the faint lingering stains were still there on the walls and floor, but obviously his mother couldn't see them or hadn't noticed. He started to smile through his tears.

"I'm sorry, Mom. I just got busy doing my homework and didn't get a chance to clean up. I'll do it first thing in the morning before school."

"You'll do it right now. Frances doesn't need to face this shambles tomorrow. She's got laundry and dusting to do. You get right downstairs and put the kitchen in order. And pick up your clothes and drop them in the hamper on the way down!"

He couldn't help smiling around the tear stains on his cheeks. She looked at him. "Oh, Christopher. Why do you have to be such a devil?" And she took him in her arms and started to hug him.

He felt the softness of her neck and smelled the light perfume she wore. It was almost nice having her hug him, but pretty soon he needed to get moving. He jumped up and while she watched with a puzzled expression on her face he hopped into his pajama pants and ran downstairs. He had never moved so quickly to do a cleanup job in his whole life. She scratched her head. Something was up, there was no doubt about it. She shrugged and went to get ready for bed.

Downstairs Christopher looked around. There wasn't a single polka dot in sight. He ran through the dining room and the living room. Except for the bath towel he had left on the floor it looked the same to him. His father sat behind the desk and looked up at him in the doorway.

"Come here," he said, and turned his chair away from the desk. Christopher lay himself across his father's knees without any argument. His father hesitated at the unexpected cooperation, then took three good wallops with his open palm. Christopher was shocked at how much it hurt through the thin pajama fabric and tried to rub some of the smarting pain away with his hands. As he did so he looked curiously up at the ceiling and the walls. The dots were all gone! He looked at his father, and his father looked back at him. He saw that no lecture was coming so he turned, still rubbing his backside, and picked up the towel as he walked back to the kitchen. He thought he saw a small blue dot go scurrying into a shadow behind the door, but when he looked closely it was gone.

He shook his head thoughtfully and started wiping up the spatters of ice cream on the floor. He remembered the letting go and the breaking feeling inside him. Carefully he sent a kind of questioning mental finger poking into that place in his head. It felt a little sore, like a strained muscle.

He put the dirty dishes and glasses into the dishwasher and then scraped half-heartedly at the burnt tomato sauce on the oven bottom. He tossed the wet bath towel into the laundry room hamper and slowly went up the back stairs to his room.

The next week seemed endless. Each day he had to go home right after school and his mother insisted he call her from the kitchen, with Frances hanging over his shoulder. Then he had to go upstairs to do his homework, make his bed if he had been too rushed to do it before he left in the morning, and then all he had left was to look out the window into the backyard where the sun sent speckled shadows through the big elm tree. He couldn't ride his bike, he couldn't play with his friends. Officially he couldn't even phone them, though he made several calls to Bill when Frances was busy in the kitchen. All he had left was television, and he found himself falling asleep every afternoon in front of the set and then lying wide-eyed looking up at the ceiling later, when his mother made him put out the light and go to bed.

Those hours in the darkness gave him lots of time to think. He still wasn't sure about what had happened during the Polka Dot Disaster. At first he thought the talisman had done something to his eyes to make the world seem covered with the dots, but then he remembered how Crackers had acted. There was no doubt the dots were real. Then he thought it was a trick of the light, but they had appeared everywhere, even under his hair on his scalp, in the shadows of the furniture, under the water of the shower.

No, they had been as real as real could be.

And they had disappeared when all his scrubbing and scurrying around had accomplished nothing!

The Headmaster called it homework. Somewhere in it there was a lesson to be learned. What had he done to make them disappear? All he could remember was the anger and fear, and the letting go that seemed to break something loose inside. Could he have done it himself? He would have liked to ask the Headmaster about it, but he wasn't about to go back to the big house again. Anyway, if he did, and if he had another talisman to bring home, he would be prepared and not panic no matter what happened.

As he drifted off to sleep at last he thought again about the lesson he had learned from the polka dots. One thing for sure, he was never again going to think polka dots were pretty.

Monday he was allowed out again and he resumed a more normal life after school with his friends, in the park or along the lake. One afternoon he rode his bike to the nearby college campus and checked the library card index for books about SQ and PQ, but all they had was stuff about IQ, which he already knew stood for Intelligence Quotient. He asked the librarian who was standing up on one of those library ladders if he knew where he could read about Sensitivity Quotient. The man looked down from his perch with a sneer.

"There is no such thing as Sensitivity Quotient, young man," and he turned back to his books. Christopher carefully tied the librarian's shoelaces to the rung of the ladder before leaving.

On his way home that evening he rode past the old house. He could see a dim light in one of the second floor windows. He wondered what the laboratories and other rooms in the house were like. If it wasn't the Headmaster's home, what could they all be used for? And where did he live? Christopher stood across the street for a few minutes, but when nothing happened he grew bored and went home.

After school the next day he didn't play ball in the schoolyard or ride his bike. He went directly to the old house and pulled the chain. When the Headmaster came to the door he said, "Right on time. Good. I'm happy to see you again, Christopher."

Christopher nodded and followed him into the library. He could see the same folder in the middle of the desk. The Headmaster really had been expecting him.

"You did your homework quite well last week so we'll move right along." He stood leaning against the front of the desk, his arms folded tightly across his chest. The arms were so thin he was able to hold the opposite shoulders with his hands.

"I want you to focus your eyes on mine and then slowly bring the focus back into the space between us so that my face will blur. At the same time you will tell me what happened when you pressed the talisman, and why."

Christopher looked at the Headmaster's eyes and felt drawn into their deep shadows. Then, with an effort, he began to pull his focus back into the space between them. He started to talk.

"It was just a game, just a silliness. You wanted to scare me a little." He found it very difficult to keep the focus on empty space. He could feel the muscles in his eyes quivering as they tried to snap back to the Headmaster's face. He went on.

"I think you were showing me what you could do," he hesitated.

"Yes, go on," Headmaster said.

"And, maybe . . . I don't know."

"Yes."

"Maybe show me what I could do."

"Right. Very good, Christopher. That was a little tricky at the end there and not so easy to see. All right. Keep the focus between us now. What do you see?"

"I don't know. Nothing. It's all a blur."

Headmaster reached to the wall beside him. "I'll be lowering the lights now. Keep the focus. You don't need to say anything anymore. Don't worry if you feel a little dizzy. Good. You've got it now. Hold it. Hold it. Hold it. Hoooooollld iiiit. . . ."

The next thing Christopher knew he was lying on the leather couch again, only this time Headmaster was sitting at his desk writing in the folder. He looked up and said, "Don't move too fast. That was excellent, Christopher. I'm very pleased with you."

He went over to the wall cabinet again and drew out a tray of talismans. "Here's your homework. You'll have to leave now. We're running a little late. The bell has already rung."

And seconds later Christopher found himself on the street walking through the late afternoon dusk and wondering again at the short/long lessons. He had the new talisman in his pocket and he knew it would have an engraved "010" on its face—a binary two, meaning his second homework assignment.

That evening was filled with schoolwork. He had put off an essay for two weeks, and his mother knew it was due the next day so she stayed with him after dinner and wouldn't let him quit until it was done. By then it was fairly late and he preferred to wait to do the Headmaster's homework at a better time.

But the next day when his English teacher was making the kids all read their essays, his thoughts drifted back to the bright library and Headmaster's deep eyes. He took the talisman out of his pocket and turned it over. Again the warmth and weight of the little cube surprised him. He held it down below the level of the desk and carefully kept his eyes on the teacher so she wouldn't think he was up to something. A girl finished reading her essay just as the bell rang, and the class erupted into the usual confusion so Christopher was able to slip the talisman into the button-down pocket of his shirt.

He carried his books to the locker in the hall and put them on the top shelf. Idly, he looked into the mirror over the wash basin and what he saw sent a shock right through him. He could feel the hairs rise on the nape of his neck. Carefully he moved across the front of the mirror. Yes, there was the wall on the other side of the hall. He could see some of the other kids walking behind him. But where was *he?* He moved right up against the mirror to block out everything, but he blocked out nothing. Hair, face, clothes, mouth, eyes. He, Christopher, just wasn't there!

For a moment he remembered the fairy tales he had read. Something about evil people—was it vampires?—who had no mirror image. Quickly he looked down at his body. There was no body! He had no hands, no legs, no chest, nothing!

But he could feel himself. And as he reached forward to the sink faucet and turned it on, he could make the water flow. But his hand was completely invisible, even to his own eyes!

He turned as he saw a classmate in the mirror. "Hey, Dave. Where you going?"

Dave looked around, puzzled. He didn't see Christopher!

Christopher held his breath as, shaking his head, Dave moved on to his next class.

Christopher closed his eyes and thought. Okay, I'm invisible. It's obviously homework oh, one, oh. I can't go to my next class and be marked present—he giggled—so I'll cut. Now, what have I always wanted to do and couldn't because . . . .

Just then a group of girls from his homeroom class appeared at the end of the hall. They were walking slowly toward him intent on their whispered conversation.

Christopher smiled gleefully to himself and stood quite still as they approached. At last he could hear them and as they walked he kept close behind.

"He is too gorgeous!" Marie was saying. "And when he moves his hips under his guitar I get shivers up my back!"

"Yeah, he's cool. What are you going to wear to the party tonight?"

[23]

Christopher stopped following. He could hear that sort of conversation anytime. He looked in at the doorway that opened to his right. It was the main school office, and the lady who worked there all the time was intent on a phone conversation with someone. Christopher slid carefully past the swinging partition so she wouldn't notice and stepped as quietly as he could around her desk and over to the principal's office. He could hear Mr. Green talking.

"One more time and I'll suspend him. I mean that. He's a smart-mouthed kid who thinks he can say and do anything he pleases. He talked back to me, he talked back to Mrs. Stout, and he acts as if he's the principal of this school. Well, he's going to find out that he is not. I mean it, George, one more problem with him and out he goes."

Christopher could hear the soft mumble of Mr. Fried's answer—he knew Mr. Fried liked and wanted to help Johnny Dawes, but Johnny spent his whole life with a chip on his shoulder. He bullied everyone in the school, and even Christopher had to let his temper show every once in a while to keep Johnny at a safe distance.

He slipped around the door and into the principal's office. Mr. Fried was just getting up from the visitor's chair to leave, so Christopher went to the window where he would be out of the way.

"Close the door, would you please, George?" Mr. Green said. "I've got a couple of tough phone calls—including one to Mrs. Dawes—to take care of."

Christopher had a moment of panic. How long was he to be locked in here with the principal? He sat quietly on the arm of the couch and listened while Mr. Green told Johnny's mother she would have to come in for another conference. Johnny wasn't in school half the time, did she know that? And he was "insubordinate, intractable, and incorrigible." It was the principal's favorite speech, and Christopher had heard it himself a couple of times. They made their appointment and then Mr. Green called his wife.

Christopher walked around to the window. He bumped a tall plant that stood on the floor, rustling its leaves. It was hard to know where your arms were when you couldn't see them. Mr. Green looked up from his conversation as the plant moved. A breeze?

Christopher was right beside Mr. Green's chair now. A small table with a water pitcher and glasses stood just to his left. He leaned forward and blew on the back of the principal's neck. Then he had to move quickly back as Mr. Green reached with his hand to see what was touching him. He swung around in his swivel chair quickly and Christopher held his breath. They couldn't have been more than six inches apart, face to face. But, of course, Mr. Green couldn't see him though he obviously suspected something. As quietly as he could Christopher reached over to the water pitcher and tipped it in the right direction. The water cascaded down into Mr. Green's lap and then the pitcher itself followed, pouring water on the front of his shirt and down his legs. Mr. Green pushed back so violently that the chair tipped under him, and suddenly he went over on his back. His legs and arms flapped helplessly in the air. Christopher could hardly believe what was happening and a kind of craziness took hold of him. Leaving Green trapped behind the chair he went over to the file cabinet and looked at the titles of the folders. Boring, boring, boring. He reached for a stack and pulled one out. A few sheets fell from between his fingers so he let the rest fall and then tossed another handful into the air. They made a wonderful snowstorm of paper fluttering through the room. He heard Mr. Green yelp.

"What's happening? MRS. FOSTER!" he bellowed.

Christopher took another handful of papers and tossed them in the air just as the door opened, and Mrs. Foster got a faceful of them. She screamed and ran. Christopher followed with another handful of papers which he threw after her. She ran out into the hall screaming, "Mr. Green's gone crazy! Help me, somebody. Help!"

Christopher now had the outer office to himself but it would not be for long. He had to stay out of the way as the crowd came running into the office to see what Mrs. Foster was yelling about.

He climbed up on top of a desk in one corner and then leaned casually against the wall, as they all ran around looking for Mr. Green who was still struggling out from behind his desk. His hair was awry, his jacket up around his ears, the water stain on his lap suspiciously like an embarrassing loss of control. The other teachers stopped short at the door and just looked at him as he glared back.

"What happened?" they chorused.

"You're asking me! Ask Mrs. Foster. She must have seen something. Has this whole place gone crazy?" He stomped into the outer office over the paper-strewn floor.

"Get the plant engineer up here, right now. Mrs. Foster, where the hell are you?" She looked around the door jamb, carefully keeping out of his line of fire.

"Right here, Mr. Green. Are you all right now?"

"All right? Of course I'm all right. Why did you throw those papers?" He tried to be controlled but there was suppressed fury in his voice.

"Why did *I* throw the papers?" A little hysteria crept into her voice again. "Why did *you?*" Christopher hated to leave, but the doorway was clear after Mrs. Foster came in, so he jumped off the desk and slipped out.

It was all he could do to keep from laughing out loud.

As he headed down the hall he decided to stop off in his homeroom where the kids would be getting their books and clothes together, ready to go home. His homeroom teacher, Mrs. Stout, was keeping tight control—with everyone sitting at their desks and not too much buzzing. He took his usual seat but didn't dare to touch any of his books because they'd look so strange moving by themselves.

Mrs. Stout looked around and said, "Anyone know where Christopher is?" She waited a beat or two and then said, "If he thinks he can cut homeroom without getting into trouble, he's in for a real surprise." There was something unusually angry in her voice, Christopher thought.

[26]

"He didn't leave the building, Mrs. Stout," his friend Bill said from the rear of the room. "His jacket is still in our locker."

"Hmmm," she said. "I wonder where he could be? Anyone go by the office last period?"

There was a general rustle as several talked at once. "There was some sort of accident there, Mrs. Stout. Mrs. Foster was shouting, and a whole crowd of teachers and kids were there."

"Yeah. Someone said Mr. Green went crazy."

"All right, kids. Settle down. Settle down. I will check, after the bell. All right, five minutes of quiet reading before dismissal." She pushed her glasses up on her forehead and rubbed her eyes. Then she made a note on the attendance record sheet and put it into the lower drawer. Christopher decided he'd get to that little matter after everyone left. Meanwhile he sat and listened to the whispering going on around him.

"Where do you suppose he is?"

"I'll bet he was in Mr. Green's office!"

"He's been acting really crazy lately."

"He always acts crazy—he ought to be put away!"

Just then the bell rang and Mrs. Stout said, "Class dismissed. See you tomorrow."

The kids jumped up and got their books together. Christopher held himself very still in the center of his seat lest someone bump into him.

A couple of the girls went over to Bill. "Where is he, do you know?"

Bill shook his head. "I talked to him before English, but that's the last I saw of him. You know Christopher, he could be anywhere."

"Well, I wouldn't mind if he never came back." Kate had a sharp edge in her voice. "If he doesn't quit teasing and hitting me, I'm going to tell."

"Aw, Kate, you know he doesn't mean anything by it." Bill came to his defense.

"I don't care whether he means it or not. I don't like it and nobody else does either!" She turned to Cindy, standing beside her. "He's just plain bad. He takes my books and never returns them. He broke my ruler hitting a baseball, and I'm really tired of having to sew my coat buttons on again and again just because he thinks it's funny to pull them off."

Bill said, "Come on, Kate. He can be real nice. You know that."

"Sure, sometimes," she said. "But the rest of the time he's so antsy and crazy I can't stand to be around him."

Bill finally gave in. "Yeah, I guess so. He's hard to be friends with, sometimes." With that, they all moved out the door.

Christopher stayed in his seat after they were gone. Mrs. Stout got her jacket from the closet and put it on. She filled her case with homework papers and, with one last look around the room, turned out the lights and went out, closing the door behind her.

He knew he would have no trouble getting out. The lock was a simple latch that always worked from the inside. But he wasn't ready to leave just yet. He went over behind Mrs. Stout's desk and pulled out the drawer that held the attendance record. Sure enough, Mrs. Stout had put a question mark in the square alongside his name. He looked closely at the record. There were four absences marked—one in red, when he had forgotten to write an excuse for himself.

He tried to erase the red mark, but it wouldn't come out and now he had left a big smudge on the record that was going to be obvious. Well, there was an easy solution to that problem. He simply folded the whole sheet up as small as he could and put it into the waste-paper basket under a bunch of other trash. When the cleaning man came he'd empty the basket and that would be the end of that.

He looked up at the blackboard where Mrs. Stout had written her assignments for the day. She'd probably be annoyed when the attendance record turned up missing. She might even get into trouble about it. Well, that was her problem.

[29]

He didn't much like what the kids said about him. He knew he teased them sometimes but it was just for fun. Why should they get so mad? And as for the books and things, it was their own fault if they lent them. He never let anybody take his favorite things.

He wasn't going to be able to carry anything home with him so he went to the door. He let the door latch behind him and headed downstairs and out to the schoolyard.

The kids had started a softball game on the playing field. As usual Johnny Dawes was pitching and throwing them so fast that most of the kids were afraid to take a swing. He struck out a player in three pitches and then sneered as he came in and picked up the bat for his turn at the plate.

"Come on," he shouted. "Give me something with a little speed on it. I'm getting tired of waiting half an hour for the ball to get here."

The pitcher was a small boy, but with strong shoulders and arms. He tossed the hair out of his eyes, wound up and underhanded a slider that headed right to Johnny's knees. Johnny stepped back half a pace and leaned down into it. The sound of the hit was clean and hard and everyone knew Johnny had another homer. He took his time tossing the bat aside and then began a slow, confident lope to first base.

Meanwhile, Fred, the kid out in center field, was running backward as fast as he could, but there was no way he would be able to get under the hit which bounced high on the back fence and rolled forward. Fred had the ball when Johnny was rounding second. If he could have thrown all the way home there was a chance they might have held Johnny at third. As it was, Fred threw to Paul at second who made a sloppy catch but turned quickly. By this time Johnny was halfway to home and running easily. He would pass right in front of Christopher, who simply couldn't resist: he put his foot out into Johnny's path. It hooked the back leg and Johnny flew into the air, legs and arms swinging wildly in the vain effort to get his balance. He landed flat on his stomach and all the wind was knocked out of him in one big "whoosh."

He just lay there, gasping and holding his stomach. All the kids came rushing over so Christopher backed out of the way. They all just stood around helplessly, and it seemed to take a long time for Johnny to get his breath. He just sat there, his face greenish, a trickle of blood drying on his lip where he had cut it.

Nobody could figure out what had happened, and somehow it didn't seem as funny as Christopher expected.

He was tempted to stop at the candy store on the way home, but then decided to skip it. For some strange reason he could feel tears beginning to fill his eyes, and he would have liked to have his mother hug him and hold him in her lap the way she used to when he was little.

He had done something wrong this time, he knew it. The Head-master would flunk him and he'd have no more adventures. He trudged home watching the ground move under him without legs or feet. He crossed the streets carefully—if he got hit, no one would ever find him or even know. He thought how his friends would feel if they never saw him again. They'd be sorry, he was sure. Well, almost sure. He guessed he wasn't a lot of fun to have around all the time. They got so mad at him when he messed up or broke things, but it wasn't his fault he was a little clumsy, was it?

He turned the corner of his block and saw his sister, Penny, sitting on the front steps by herself. She wasn't usually home this early and as he came close he noticed that she was crying. She wasn't sobbing or anything, but just looking down the front path with tears rolling down her cheeks. Her school books were on the steps beside her and on top of them an open letter.

Curious, he came up beside her and twisted around so he could read the letter. When he did, he felt as Johnny must have when the ground came up and socked him in the pit of the stomach.

The letter read:

Dear Penny,

Thank you very much for the invitation to your pajama party next Saturday. I've talked it over with my mom and some of the other girls and we think that maybe we'd better not come. It's not you. You're really super and if you can come to my house, Mom says we can have it here.

I haven't wanted to tattle, but when we were at your house last month Christopher ruined my dress with that supposedly disappearing ink, and the mousetrap in our sleeping bags wasn't funny at all. He just won't leave us alone and unless your mother or father are home we'll be sure to get into another fight.

Everybody feels the same, so why don't we have the pajama party at my house this Saturday? Please come and bring your records.

Marge

Penny took a little ball of tissue out of her purse and blotted her face. She gave a big sigh and then tore the letter up into tiny pieces. She didn't seem angry or sad or anything. Just sort of resigned. She went around to the kitchen door.

Christopher took her place on the front porch steps and looked down the path. He felt sadness well up inside of him and a sob choked his throat. The pain and tightness grew until he couldn't stand it anymore, and then that same breaking loose feeling exploded inside and without surprise he watched his hands slowly come back into view. He shivered in the cold and headed back around to the kitchen door.

Everyone was home for dinner that night, but both Christopher and Penny were unusually quiet. They didn't fight over the last piece of pie or even argue when their mother made them do the dishes together. Penny never said a word about the letter and Christopher didn't either. After the dishes were done they went to their own rooms and didn't even say goodnight to their parents who were watching television in the family room.

After the news his mother stopped at his door. "Christopher?" she called quietly. He had turned out the light and pretended to be asleep. He let her go without a word.

Christopher was too ashamed to go to the Headmaster's the next day, but the day after he found himself walking down the same weed-grown path and pulling on the rusty chain.

The Headmaster greeted him with a nod, no smile this time, turned without speaking and led the way to the library. "Not much fun, being invisible, hmm?" he said.

Christopher shrugged. "It doesn't have anything to do with being invisible. It's just that I'm not winning any popularity contests around town these days."

"Did you ever?" The Headmaster wasn't letting him get away with anything.

"No." He didn't know what else to say.

"Do you know why?"

He was beginning to be sorry he came, sorry he ever met the Headmaster. "I don't care. They're all so boring. All they ever think about is themselves and their precious *things*." He could feel the anger rising. "They need me to bring a little excitement into their lives."

The Headmaster kept looking at him. "Penny, too?" he asked.

"Especially Penny." He remembered her crying on the front steps of their house. "She's such a pill. A big sister is about the worst thing a kid can have."

"Yes. I see. Well, we don't seem to be making much progress there but I knew we'd have that to deal with. Let's hold off awhile."

All of which made no sense at all to Christopher.

The Headmaster went around behind the desk and looked at the blue folder. "All right," he said with a smile. "No more sleeping in class. From here on we work together. Let's go into the laboratory."

Christopher felt himself tighten up. They went down a short hall and into the next room. It was the strangest laboratory Christopher had ever seen, and he had seen plenty on television and in schools. In one corner a couch and a chair stood comfortably close with a low coffee table in front of them. The facing wall was shiny white with little glistening bubbles in the surface that gave it a glow. Along one sidewall a waist-high counter held electric measuring instruments—he could recognize an oscilloscope and a chart recorder, but there were dozens of others with knobs and dials that looked very scientific.

"Sit in the chair over there, Christopher," the Headmaster said, pointing to a swivel chair in the middle of the room. He went to a storage cabinet and pulled out a large, round piece of plate glass. It was obviously heavy, and the Headmaster slid it carefully onto the coffee table. From the cabinet he also took a soft cloth and a small metal ball the size of a marble. He gave the ball to Christopher and then quickly dusted off the plate glass. Then he sat opposite Christopher on the couch.

"The plate glass has been ground smooth and completely flat. Put the ball on it, and I'll show you something."

Christopher set the ball in the center of the glass and leaned back in his chair. Then they just sat there, Christopher looking at the ball, the Headmaster looking at Christopher. Suddenly Christopher thought he saw the ball move. It rocked a little, back and forth, and

[35]

then it rolled slowly toward the edge of the glass. He thought it was going to roll off when, just at the edge, it stopped and started to roll back. Christopher raised his eyes. Was the table rocking? It certainly didn't seem to be, but now the ball was rolling back across the center of the glass and toward the other edge. Again it stopped just short and started back at a different angle. It was crazy. The ball started rolling around the outer edge of the glass, at first slowly and then more quickly as it made smaller and smaller circles. Finally it reached the center and then just stayed there; but it was spinning at high speed which Christopher could see as the surface flashed under the light.

He looked up at the Headmaster and could see the smile. "Pretty good, huh? Okay, look at me but focus in the space between us." It was a little easier this time and he could feel the Headmaster's deep eyes filling him with something, he wasn't sure what.

"Now you try. Take hold of the ball with your mind and see if you can make it move."

He had built up a lot of respect for the Headmaster over the last couple of weeks, but this was too much. He let his eyes focus on the thin face in front of him.

"Stop that!" the Headmaster said sharply. "You're here to work, not look at the scenery. Now put your mind on the ball and let's see what you can do."

Christopher looked hard at the ball and wrinkled up his forehead in a concentrated effort to move the ball, but it just sat there stubbornly. He strained and strained, looking inside himself for whatever muscles needed to be pushed. Still it sat there, mocking him. Finally, in a fury of frustration, he gave up with a snort.

"You used a magnet, didn't you?" he said.

"No," the Headmaster said quietly. "Stop trying to push the ball around. Get inside it. *Be* the ball with a desire to roll, to come closer, to explore that sheet of glass. At the same time I want you to be aware of me. Let me help you."

Christopher relaxed back into the chair a little and imagined what it was like to be a steel ball. He was perfect and round, shiny and smooth. He could feel the glass under him and had a sense of the roundness of his body. With just a small inclination of his head he could move forward. It took so little effort! Yes, it moved. He moved. The ball rocked forward a few degrees, and then a little more, and then it was easy. He rolled forward, picking up speed until he found himself heading for the edge and going too fast to stop. It was too fast! And with a jerk he leaned back and tried to stop. It was too late. The ball started to skid and it slid off the glass and onto the floor.

He reached down to pick it up when the Headmaster said, "Leave it." And then, watching in amazement, Christopher saw the ball float freely up from the floor and back onto the plate glass where it rested comfortably. Even more amazing, he had stayed with the ball in his mind and he knew how it felt to move, to rise gently and then land as delicately as a feather on the glass.

"Not bad. Try it again with a little more control this time."

And for half an hour Christopher rolled the ball in more and more complex patterns on the glass. It was the most fun he had had since attending the circus last winter. He could feel the growing sureness in him as he sensed the weight and shape of the ball to his very fingertips. Around and around it rolled, stopping in midrun and skidding slightly as he changed direction and reversed. He rolled out to the very edge of the glass and then darted it back across the middle. At one point he tried to lift the ball off the glass but the Headmaster held him down. He could feel the heavy weight of the man's mind restraining him with effortless assurance.

"You're not ready for that just yet. That ball is a lethal weapon when it flies. Just keep it on the glass for now."

But toward the end of the hour they began to experiment with other objects. Christopher was able to flip the pages of a book lying on the workshelf almost with no effort at all. The trick was to move

himself from page to page quickly and, if anything, he was afraid of
being too rough and of tearing the sheet out of the book. At the end
he slid a glass paperweight more than six inches along the counter,

and would have taken it farther, when suddenly he felt the Headmaster leave him and the power was gone.

"It was you, all the time, wasn't it?" He felt let down when he realized it had all been the Headmaster's doing.

"Not entirely. You've got some power there, but it's much too weak right now, so I helped. I want you to practice a lot this week on your own. The talisman will help get you started."

They went back to the library, and the Headmaster found the talisman marked "011." "Try not to get into trouble, please. We have no time for childish tantrums now."

The chime sounded and Christopher found himself on the street. He couldn't keep from running down the sidewalk, almost flying. For the first time since he had met the Headmaster he felt he was doing something instead of having things done to him. The sense of being in control, no matter how little, sent a charge through him that had him laughing and swinging at the bushes and trees thick with leaves. His assignment was no mystery this time. He'd need a time and place where he was sure to be by himself. That meant late at night, in his room.

He was too wound up to eat dinner, which was a mistake because Frances was convinced he was sick and called his mother. When she got home, his mother fussed over him until he lost his temper and called her a name, which got him a swat on his rear end and a cold dismissal to his room. Being a kid was such a bore!

He showered and got into bed early which convinced his mother that he had a major disease like scarlet fever or measles; but when she checked his temperature and touched his face he was cool and his eyes were clear. Shaking her head, she said goodnight; but she made Crackers get off his bed before she went out, leaving a glass of milk and a plate of chocolate chip cookies beside him.

It took hours for the house to quiet down. Crackers jumped back up on the bed as soon as the door was closed, and Christopher found himself whispering into the floppy ear, "I can do it, Crackers! I know I can! I moved that ball as easy as anything. Just you wait till

[39]

everyone's asleep and I'll show you. I'll bet I don't even need the talisman."

But when he tried, later, it didn't work. He sat back in the half darkness of his room and concentrated on the open school book on his desk. He tried to flip a page as he had done at the Headmaster's, but as hard as he tried he couldn't get it to move. Finally he took the talisman and squeezed gently. Almost at once he felt the difference. There was a place inside his head that opened up and spilled out light. He looked at the book and lifted a page almost without trying this time. He ruffled Crackers' fur and then flapped his ears. The poor dog snapped and scratched at himself and then started to bark so Christopher quit. He didn't want anyone coming to see what was wrong. He rolled a softball around the floor, but Crackers jumped down and chased it and again he was afraid the noise would wake someone.

But after a few minutes the power was gone. He could feel it go almost like a light going out. He tried to open the door in his head that released the power, but it wouldn't budge and he knew what the Headmaster meant when he said he needed a lot of practice. That was okay. He knew he could do it and he'd practice a thousand hours a day if he needed to, to be able to move things that way!

He carefully hid the talisman under the mattress and then took a long time to fall asleep.

Every night for the rest of that week Christopher practiced. He used only the smallest of pressures each time because he wanted to do as much on his own as possible. By the fifth day he was really comfortable with the power. He could control small objects easily—move them in the air, turn them, send them flying at great speed across the room, stop them in an instant. He could pick up a heavy book, too, though that took more effort and tired him, so he spent more time practicing control than strength. Soon he was able to move things even without the talisman, though with nowhere near the control he had when he had squeezed it.

But now the talisman seemed to be changing color, and he began to worry that it would lose its power before he had learned the lesson. He decided he'd take one last "field trip." After school on Friday he left his books in the locker and went over to Main Street. He squeezed the talisman as hard as he could and then roamed along the storefronts and looked in the windows. Occasionally with his mind he would twitch the sleeve of a coat or dress in a store display, and he carefully lifted a gold necklace off its black velvet pad and then hung it on the ear of a plastic head in a jeweler's window.

At Whelan's drugstore on the corner he drifted through the aisles of shampoo, hair spray, and toothpaste without interest. He tried on a pair of sunglasses, but they were too big and made him look like a visitor from outer space. The toy department had some stuff for little kids and he poked around in the stack of boxed games, but it was the usual mixture of checkers, chess, and Monopoly.

He stood and watched a white-coated pharmacist behind a high counter. The man was carefully filling a small brown bottle from one of those beakers with lines engraved on the sides. Christopher reached out with his mind and gently nudged the little bottle to one side so that the medicine spilled down the sides of the bottle and all over the man's hand. It was a pink, sticky stuff, and the man swore under his breath and then quickly looked around to see if anyone had heard him. Christopher gave him a wide grin, and the man angrily dropped the bottle into the wastebasket beside him.

"Eddy!" the man shouted.

"Yeah?" A kid of about seventeen leaned out from behind a row of shelves. He was standing on a ladder, arranging cans on a shelf.

"Run downstairs and get me a case of the pediatric erythro-mycin."

Christopher saw that Eddy held a can of baby powder in his left hand and a duster in his right. He reached out with his mind and loosened the cap of the can; then with all his might he squeezed the sides of the can together. It was much more than he had hoped for. The top of the can popped off and a great cloud of powder erupted with a "whoosh."

[41]

Eddy dropped the can as if it were burning his fingers and flew back off the ladder, right into a big hamper full of sponges. A woman walking down the same aisle screamed as she saw the white cloud of powder moving toward her. She started backing away, still screaming in short shrieks, so Christopher took hold of one of her heels with his mind and just held it on the floor with the slightest of pressures. It was enough. The woman, arms flailing, her mouth still gaping, went right into a tall basket of rubber balls which promptly spilled out and started rolling all over the floor.

The pharmacist came running out from behind his counter to see what was going on. Christopher now rounded up all the balls with his mind and herded them toward the pharmicist in a rolling wave. The pharmacist looked at all the balls coming toward him with amazed horror. He leaped up in the air trying to get over them but there was no chance, and with a wild shout he landed right in the middle of them. His legs were pumping like a mouse in a spinning cage and for a couple of seconds it looked as if he were going to make it, but then with a despairing shout the man went headfirst into the shelves, sweeping stacks of candy before him.

A big, redfaced, beefy man whom Christopher knew as the security guard came running out of the office in the rear of the store. Christopher gathered all the rubber balls together again and started them down the aisle toward the man. He stopped and looked at the balls rolling and bouncing toward him. His eyes opened wide and he started to back away slowly holding his hands out as if to stop them. Christopher kept them rolling and bouncing, and when they reached the man's feet he had them roll over his shoes and up his legs. The man screamed and started frantically brushing the clinging balls away from his body and legs.

Christopher could feel the tight wildness in his chest as the power surged through him. People were shouting and trying to help the security guard get the rubber balls off, but when they pushed one loose Christopher just popped it back as if it were on an elastic

[42]

band. The guard was whimpering now as he brushed weakly at the balls which had moved up his body and were now clustered around his head and neck.

And then suddenly they all dropped free as Christopher felt a clamp move in on his mind. A voice thundered in his ears so loud he closed his eyes and clasped his hands to his ears.

"CHRISTOPHER!" It was the Headmaster. The voice rang in his head. It seemed to echo from side to side. He felt a rough thrust at the back of his head which threw him forward onto his knees.

"HOW DARE YOU!" It was so loud it made his head ache. He curled up into a ball and started to cry.

"HOW DARE YOU!" The same outraged fury in Headmaster's voice. He was pulled up to his feet and shaken like a dusty mop.

"PUT IT ALL BACK. AT ONCE!" Christopher scrambled to pick up the balls that had rolled all over the store. The other customers just stood and looked at him as he started jerking around like a marionette at the end of a string, picking up cans of powder and bars of candy and rushing to put them on their shelves. He helped Eddy climb out of the basket of sponges and dabbed ineffectually at the powder that coated his face and hair.

"It's all right. I'm all right, kid." Eddy said. They stood and looked at the security guard whose face was pale, his hands shaking uncontrollably.

"I'm sorry," Christopher said. The security guard looked at him but it was obvious he didn't see him. Slowly his eyes began to clear. He rubbed his face hard and it was as if he were coming back from some far-off place.

Everyone started to wander off, back about their business, not understanding and not even talking much. Christopher left the store feeling weak in his legs, with sweat popping wet on his back and chest. He remembered the fury in the Headmaster's voice and he knew it was all over. He'd ruined the first good thing that had happened to him in years. Why did he keep doing that? Every time things started going well he just seemed to get into trouble. Was he really a bad kid the way everyone seemed to think? He hated himself. He hated the way people looked at him sometimes. He hated when the teachers in school yelled at him because he couldn't understand something. He hated when the kids got mad at him or when his dad got that exasperated, end-of-patience look.

But now it was ruined. He reached out with his mind and flipped a paper cup up into the air end over end. He'd never be able to do what the Headmaster could do with that steel ball. He'd never see the other rooms in the old house and get other powers he hadn't even dreamed of. What was the use? The whole world was against him and it was right.

Across Main Street a woman and a little kid came out of a bookstore. The kid was playing with a small red ball, throwing it into the air and catching it. But he was only about five years old, and catching it wasn't always easy. His mother was stuffing something back into her purse and she held a paper bag under her arm.

When they were getting close to the street the kid threw the ball, and when it fell it hit his fingertips and bounced away from him right out into the street. Out of the corner of his eye Christopher could see that a car was coming and, with that certainty you get sometimes, he knew what was going to happen.

The kid went out after the ball without a glance in either direction. The mother didn't see him, her eyes still on her purse. The car was moving fairly fast, and the driver didn't see the kid dart out between parked cars.

It was all happening so clearly in front of Christopher. For one split second he was going to shout and then, realizing that it wouldn't do a bit of good, he reached out with his mind and, with all the power he could bring to bear, pressed down on the car's brake pedal.

Thank God! They were power brakes, or he couldn't possibly have had the strength. The brakes grabbed, the wheels locked, and the tires screeched on the pavement. It was still all in slow motion to Christopher. The woman heard the screech, looked up quickly and reached out for the kid, but she was way too late. The kid looked up at the car and froze as it skidded toward him. The driver saw the kid and lifted his foot off the gas pedal and pressed on the brake. Christopher could feel the extra pressure the driver was adding.

It takes thirty feet of full braking to stop a car going twenty miles an hour, and the kid was about twenty-five feet from the car when Christopher hit the brakes. He could see that the kid would still be hit, maybe run over, so now that the driver had his foot on the brake pedal Christopher shifted his attention to the kid. He didn't have the strength to move fifty pounds of boy, but he could kick his feet out from under him and push him so that he fell toward the middle of the car, between the wheels.

Sure enough, the car shuddered to a stop with its front bumper over the kid's face.

And then there were about five seconds of absolute silence. No one on the street moved. The woman had her mouth open ready to scream. The driver stared through the windshield, thinking he had killed the kid. The kid looked up at the underside of the car.

Christopher pulled his mind back and just watched.

Of course for him it was all anticlimax. The woman ran out and grabbed the kid from under the car. The kid started to scream in fear. The driver jumped out of the car and ran forward. They didn't know he hadn't been touched, and the kid probably didn't know what was going on himself. Anyway, he was screaming so loud there was no room in his mouth for explanations.

It began to be funny. Christopher started to laugh, when he heard the voice again.

"Very good, Christopher." It was the Headmaster speaking very quietly. "But you had better not laugh or those people will beat the stuffing out of you.

"That counts, but we're not through with the drugstore. Now go home and take it easy. You'll find you're a little tired. You had better think about it all, and I'll see you Monday."

Christopher stood frozen to the spot, staring sightlessly at the noisy crowd gathering around the car, the woman, and the still-screaming kid. He had never done anything like that before and it was kind of a good feeling. Especially good because no one knew, so they weren't making a big fuss over him; but he knew, and it was a delicious secret. It was even better to know that the door in his head had opened and stayed open—just a crack maybe, but it wasn't locked shut again now that the power had worn off.

He ran all the way home in an easy lope. "All right, Headmaster. I'm thinking about it," he said out loud to the bush in front of his house. He ran up the steps to the front porch and then jumped high over the railing—and landed heavily in his mother's petunia patch.

The bush shook its top with a little help from Christopher's mind as he went in for dinner.

The weekend went on and on. Christopher sat glued in front of the television set that night, his mind a tired blank. Desperate for something to distract him, he got his mother to let him paint the garage door and spent an hour slopping half a gallon of white paint on the door, on the bushes nearby, and on himself. Then, leaving the paint, brushes, and ladder in front of the garage, he went over to the schoolyard to show his friends his smeared face.

But there was no one there except for a bunch of little kids throwing baskets on the basketball court. He bought a soft ice cream cone at the corner stand and, dripping, went exploring. He liked roaming through the hardware store but was shooed out of a women's dress shop. He went to the bank and wrote his name and savings account number on a bunch of bank deposit slips and slipped them back in the stack for unwary customers. When he came out of the bank he hopped on a bus waiting at the corner and stayed on all the way into town, with his face pressed against the window and his sticky fingers keeping other riders away from the seat beside him.

For some reason the store owners weren't all that happy to see his smeared face and paint-spattered pants come through their doors, so he found himself pressed to buy or leave, which left no time for the kind of browsing that he liked. One interesting thing about the power, however, was that he could reach out and touch things with his mind in a way that was much more informative than he ever got from his fingers. He stood outside a pawnshop window and was able to feel the shapes and edges of the guns, knives, coins, tools, and other fascinating things without having to ask permission. He got into trouble only when he plucked one of the strings of a guitar, and the store owner came rushing over to the window and stared at him angrily. Christopher looked back at him, raised his arms comically, shrugged his shoulders, and went on down the street.

At a hot dog stand he mentally pinched a fat woman's behind while she was stuffing her face with a frankfurter piled high with onions, tomatoes, pickles, and mustard. She jumped a foot off the stool and looked around accusingly at everyone but Christopher, who was all the way on the other side of the stand.

On the bus going home he kept flipping the coins in the bus driver's coin box and even managed to bounce one right out through the small slot at the top, which so amazed the driver he pulled over to the next bus stop and spent ten minutes examining the thing. He said it had to be broken because it was impossible for the coins to get out otherwise.

In other words, it was just another ordinary, boring Saturday with nothing to do.

Sunday was even worse with the stores mostly closed and the whole family busy with their own projects. He and Bill played on the rocks by the lake and they both fell in and came home sopping wet and bedraggled. They dripped puddles all the way up the back stairs to Christopher's room and dropped their wet clothes in an untidy pile in one corner while they snapped the damp towels at each other's bare bottoms. But, much as he liked Bill, he couldn't tell him about the Headmaster; and so it was a relief to see him go home when it got dark.

He was going to cut classes Monday but couldn't think of anything he wanted to do except go to Headmaster's, and he knew his appointment wasn't until after school. So he dragged himself through the day, minute by endless minute, until at last the final bell rang and he was free. He was out of the classroom like a shot and pulled on the rusty chain at the old house on Sheridan Road just seconds later. It seemed to take a long time for the door to be answered; and for a moment he caught his breath, thinking that maybe no one was home.

But finally the Headmaster opened the door. He just stood there looking at Christopher without much welcome in his face. "You're a little early," he said. "You can come in and wait, but I may be a few minutes."

Christopher just nodded. The Headmaster led him to a chair in the front hall. "Sit here. Don't go wandering around." He looked hard at Christopher and then went to the library and closed the door.

Christopher could hear murmuring voices through the door. He was sorely tempted to listen but was afraid the Headmaster would know. He tried turning the doorknob with his mind, but found it too stiff; so instead he closed his eyes and tried to spread his ears and interpret what was being said.

Christopher felt as if he were just on the edge of understanding— at one point he was sure he heard the Headmaster say his name— but that was the best he could do. In a few minutes the voices stopped and the Headmaster came to the door and called him in.

"We'll be working in another laboratory this afternoon, but we'd better have a talk first." That was both encouraging and unnerving at the same time.

"I'm not your parent, Christopher, and I have no intention of taking that role or providing elementary parental controls." He paused. "By that I mean simply that it isn't my responsibility to teach you not to harm another human being. I can't think of anything that anyone in this world has done to you that merits the way

[50]

you treat them. Teasing, lying, cheating, hurting another living entity—either physically or mentally—we do not do. If you do it again, and rest assured I will know of it, then you can forget about me and whatever latent powers you may have. I don't need you, Christopher. There are others with many of the same potentialities that you have, and they may be quicker learners and less trouble."

He stopped, but the stern glare in his eyes did not soften. "I don't like lectures. It isn't the way I teach and I suspect that it isn't the way you learn. But I will make this threat. If you abuse any of the powers you learn here you will regret it for the rest of your life—the rest of your life."

They stood looking at each other, and Christopher could feel the tears filling his eyes. He could have put up a good act for almost anyone else, but he couldn't say a word to the Headmaster. He just nodded his head, flicked the water out of his eyes, and looked back as straight as he knew how.

"All right. Let's go." They went out of the library to a door just a few steps away. The Headmaster opened it and Christopher looked in. He could see a long hall with another door at the far end. It was painted a bright yellow.

"You'll be on your own here. Just go down that hall and through the yellow door." Christopher turned and went into the hall.

"Just a minute. Let me help you get started." He looked into Christopher's eyes, and again Christopher could feel the power flowing into him. It was stronger and clearer this time than ever before, perhaps because they were so close that their noses were almost touching.

"All right. Off you go. I'll be seeing you in a little while."

Christopher stepped through the door into the long hall, and the Headmaster closed it behind him. While there seemed to be nothing difficult about the assignment, Christopher decided to be very careful. He stood and looked at everything around him. There wasn't too much to see. The hall was about six feet wide and seemed about thirty feet long. It was curious that there were no doors along the sides, but there were framed paintings along the walls on either side. A narrow, cushioned bench stood against the right sidewall about halfway to the far door, and another one stood on the opposite side farther along. Within reach on his left, there stood against the wall a narrow, wooden table with a silver plate in its center and a white card on the plate. He moved forward a couple of steps and looked at the card. The message printed on the card simply said, "Walk, do not run."

Christopher dropped the card and, shrugging, started down the hall. Almost at once he sensed that something was wrong. His perspective shifted and the hall suddenly seemed quite different. By the time he had taken two steps past the table his head touched the ceiling, and when he looked back he realized that the table was much smaller at this end than the other!

He turned back and went quickly to his starting point. When he turned and looked down the length of the hall it was quite normal— the table on his left, the benches farther down, the yellow door facing him. He edged forward very slowly this time and noticed that the ceiling was definitely curving downward and the walls were slanted in on the sides. The table was much smaller at one end than it was on the other.

He crouched down and continued forward into the passage, but the ceiling touched his head again, forcing him down on his hands and knees. By the time he reached the first cushioned bench, the walls on either side were almost touching his shoulders!

In fact all the distances had become so small that he could reach forward and touch the second bench. It stood only about one inch high, and the yellow door at the end of the hall was obviously only large enough for someone no taller than his little finger!

How was he ever to get down the hall and through the door?

Carefully Christopher backed away on his hands and knees until he reached the large end again. He sat on the floor with his back against the door. It was amazing. From this end the hall looked

perfectly straight and the far door looked as big as the one he was leaning against. But he knew that it was all an illusion of some kind.

He looked at it helplessly. He wasn't about to go back out through the door behind him. That would be giving up. But how was he to get through that little door? He was much too big to fit. He had to make the door bigger, that was all.

He tested his power by extending his mental fingers to flip the card on the silver plate. The power was there and working well. He reached forward with his mind then, and tried to enlarge the hall in front of him. He could feel the resistance. He had never tried to handle anything even as heavy as a lamp or table; how was he to move the walls and ceiling?

Again he tried, and this time really projected the power until the sweat popped out on his forehead. Still nothing moved, and when he crawled forward cautiously he found that the ceiling sloped down as quickly as before.

There had to be some other way. The Headmaster wasn't likely to teach him the same thing twice. If he couldn't change the dimensions of the hall, he had to do something else. And then it came to him in one of those clear flashes: if he couldn't change the dimensions of the hall, it was because the assignment was to change himself!

He could almost see the Headmaster nodding in approval. He closed his eyes and reached into his body, sensing his chest, his arms, his hips, and down through his legs. Then, with a kind of squeezing action in his mind, he began to compress everything—not with pressure from outside but with a kind of internal withdrawal. He knew it was working even before he opened his eyes, and when he did, he saw with satisfaction that the table was now at the level of his eyes and the door behind him seemed almost twice as big as it had before. He started to walk forward now and was able to reach the first cushioned bench and sit on it comfortably.

Looking back, the table and door seemed quite normal. Looking forward, it was the same. But as he stood and walked on, once again the ceiling touched his head before he had taken two steps. He stopped, closed his eyes, and again concentrated on pulling inward, shrinking his body.

He opened his eyes and found he had made another good adjustment. The first cushioned bench was higher than the top of his head, and the hall behind him seemed enormous. He walked forward toward the next bench, and when he reached it found it was just the right size.

He sat and looked around him. It was interesting that, when he had adjusted his size to suit where he was in the hall, everything looked normal. Just a few steps now to the yellow door. But again the ceiling quickly sloped down and the walls came in to touch his shoulders. He crouched down, but this time kept his eyes open as he reached into his body and pulled it tight one last time. Now he could see the walls move up around him. He took two steps forward and took the door handle, which was exactly the right size. He pushed the door open and cautiously looked out.

At once he sensed he was in a vast space. The floor underfoot was a single, enormous plank of wood. On his right a thin plastic pipe slanted up from where it was embedded in a coarse stone base. To his left he saw a large but obviously artificial plateau. It was as high as his head, and its cliff face seemed to be made up of dozens of layers of a thin woody material of some kind. Just then he heard a deep, thunderous rumbling and he felt a strong breeze on his face that smelled of new-mown grass.

He looked up and saw an enormous hand falling toward him. He was about to turn and run when he recognized where he was. The hand stopped just a few feet in front of him and held a white board that seemed to be about four feet high and eight feet long. On the board in hand printed characters he read the message the Headmaster had written.

"Very good, Christopher. That was the quickest anyone has ever done it. Now, slowly come back to normal or you'll hurt yourself."

Christopher looked up beyond the hand and saw the Headmaster looking down at him. He was on the Headmaster's desk. The plastic tube was a fountain pen in a marble base that looked like a huge block of stone. The cliff to his left was a book, its pages like layers of wood stacked high. The rumbling thunder was the Headmaster's voice—much too low in frequency for his tiny ears to hear.

Christopher took a deep breath and felt his body expand. Soon he could sit comfortably on the book, and then he looked around at the desk. He was still too small to be able to talk to the Headmaster, but it was fascinating to see the things on the desk from this perspective. The papers were like enormous sheets of wood, the lamp was as tall as a mountain, and its light was much more red than yellow. He could see the Headmaster's face clearly now with the deeply socketed eyes. He sensed the Headmaster's impatience, and so he continued to grow until he was big enough to jump off the desk to the floor and was soon back to his normal size.

[55]

"Since you came through so quickly, I'm going to dismiss you early today." The Headmaster was smiling at him for the first time, and Christopher was surprised at how proud it made him feel. "Here's the next talisman. I want you to practice this week and work on the telekinesis as well. I have a report to make that will keep me off this . . . " he paused, " . . . out of town for a few days. So I won't see you again until late next week. You'll know when.

"One thing about the shrinking. As you know, there are limits to the size you can reach—physical limits established by the size of atoms and molecules and the wavelength of light. So don't waste time trying to get yourself any smaller than you were here. Also you may find some unexpected dangers in the flora and fauna when you're that size, so always be prepared to get back to normal, and quickly."

With no more than that, Christopher found himself out on the street, the talisman with "100" engraved on its side in his pocket, and the sense of having been good at something for once in his life.

For the rest of the week he kept the new talisman under the loose floorboard in the attic. He wasn't in a hurry to have any new adventures for a while and thought this one might be dangerous, so he wanted to be sure to have lots of time when his mother wouldn't worry.

Early Saturday afternoon he was ready. His mother had spent the morning out in the garden trimming bushes, cutting flowers, and planting bulbs. Then she changed to a dress and persuaded his father to go with her to town to shop. Penny was off with her friends. Christopher looked around the house for a good place; then decided to try the backyard where there were grass and bushes and all sorts of living things. He took a hatpin from his mother's dresser and, making sure that Crackers wouldn't be able to follow him, went out the back door to the patio. He held the gold cube between thumb and middle finger and squeezed hard.

The effect was almost instantaneous. Within just a few seconds he was no taller than a ballpoint pen, standing on patio bricks which seemed as big as Ping-Pong tables. As he expected, the hatpin hadn't changed in size, so it made a good walking stick as he jumped from brick to brick and made his way to the flower bed alongside the house. The ground was rough and lumpy where his mother had turned and broken up the soil. Under one lump he saw something that brought him up short. It was a monstrous slug oozing its way along and leaving a trail of greasy film behind it. It seemed to sense his presence because it stopped for a second and the blind head lifted, and the two short antennae, like ears on its head, scanned its surroundings. Christopher stood very still, holding the hatpin like a rifle across his chest and ready for anything. But the slug dropped its head and started working its way back under the turned earth.

Christopher climbed up the waist-high ridge that marked the beginning of the lawn and pushed through the grass. The grass was as tall as his shoulder, but there was plenty of space between the blades so that he could move easily, though he had to keep his eyes on the ground which was often uneven and littered with rounded stones.

Striding quickly through a sparse section and looking from side to side, he suddenly found himself face to face with a large black ant. It stopped, too, then moved forward with its bent antenna probing for him; and he backed off quickly, swinging the hatpin like a bat and striking the ant's big, faceted eye with the rounded head of the pin. The blow knocked the ant sideways, but it recovered quickly and with its six legs churning disappeared in the grass.

Not liking the limited visibility in the grass, Christopher turned back toward the flower bed. A spider hung from a low bush where it was busily repairing a web that reached from a branch to the ground beneath. New white thread seemed to unwind from a hole in the bottom of the spider's body, and it was fascinating to see how skillfully the spider used its legs to weave the new thread with the old.

While it was still an ugly beast with a fat, obscene abdomen, its grace with the thin bent legs made a wonderful show. Just then Christopher heard a heavy thumping on the ground behind him, and as he turned he saw an enormous squirrel moving toward him. He stayed quite still, but obviously the squirrel had seen him and was coming over to take a look.

Christopher lifted the hatpin and stood his ground as the squirrel stopped just a few feet away and then sat up on its hind legs and stared.

"Never saw one like me, huh?" Christopher said. The squirrel cocked its head to one side and looked at him out of one eye for all the world as if it understood what he had said. It leaned forward, just out of arm's reach, and wriggled its nose.

Christopher gently touched the nose with the round end of the hatpin. "Don't let's get too nosy, okay?"

The squirrel sat back quickly and rubbed its nose with its front paws.

"I know what you want," Christopher said. "Come here." His mother would be furious if she knew, but Christopher figured this was an emergency. He climbed up the flower bed and then, seeing a small mound that his mother left, started throwing the clumps of earth to one side. It was slow work but the squirrel just sat there looking at him with its head tilted in a comical way.

Christopher looked at it. "You're not going to help, are you? Okay. I guess I'll manage." It was easy to move the soft clumps of earth, and soon he had cleared a hole almost waist deep. By this time the squirrel was getting a little more interested. Its nose was twitching like mad and it came very close. Christopher uncovered the top of a flower bulb and then climbed out of the hole.

"See? Try it. I'll bet it's a new taste sensation."

The squirrel came quickly to the edge of the hole and then, with three or four quick swipes of its front paws, it uncovered the bulb his mother had planted and held it up to its mouth. In tiny nibbling bites, it stripped the outer surface by turning the small bulb in its

[59]

two front paws. Christopher sat back and watched as the squirrel ate the bulb and then licked its paws. When it finished, it stopped quite still and looked at Christopher as if to say, "Wonderful, do you know where any more of these might be buried?"

"You'd better be satisfied with that because my mom would have both our tails if she knew I was showing it to you." The squirrel suddenly seemed to freeze and then in one bound it leaped for the bushes and scrabbled up the side of the house.

"Huh?" Christopher said. "Where you going in such a hurry?" He looked around and then gasped. A big, mangy cat was standing in the shadows looking at him with its head down and great amber eyes staring. The black irises were like two exclamation points glittering at him. Christopher took a step back without thinking and tripped and fell. The cat moved forward eagerly. Many times he had seen this same cat running through the bushes with a mouse or bird in its mouth. It was a quick and merciless hunter, silent as the night and afraid of nothing.

Christopher stood quickly and decided he'd better get himself back to full size before this cat got the wrong idea. He backed very slowly and closed his eyes when suddenly he heard the cat make the loudest, most bloodcurdling scream he had ever heard.

His eyes flew open to see the squirrel astride the cat's back, fending off its biting teeth with its front paws! The cat rolled quickly on its back, eyes wide with outrage and fury. A squirrel attacking a cat! Impossible! It recovered and leapt forward, but it was a hair's breadth too late. The squirrel scampered across the grass, the cat leaping after it. In one bound the squirrel jumped four feet up the tree and within seconds was high up on the branches scolding in that nasty, nasal way squirrels do. The cat had scrabbled up a few feet but was no match for the squirrel in a tree.

Christopher slowly backed under the bush. The squirrel had risked its own life to save him. It was hard to believe.

The cat sniffed and then dropped to the ground and strolled away as if nothing had happened. Certainly it wouldn't admit the squirrel's noisy chatter had anything to do with him.

The squirrel jumped from the tree to the roof of the house and then nimbly down to the bush near Christopher. There was a gleam in its eye, and Christopher could have sworn he saw a grin at the side of the mouth.

"Thanks, friend," he said. But the squirrel turned quickly and disappeared in the bushes.

Christopher waited a few minutes and then took that deep breath that would bring him back to normal size in a few seconds. He slipped the talisman out of his pocket and looked at it. He wasn't always crazy about the assignments the Headmaster gave him, and while being small was interesting it wasn't his favorite way to be.

Suddenly there were so many great things to do he never wanted the days to end. When his mother made him turn out the light at night, he would lie with his eyes wide open staring at the ceiling, unable to go to sleep. It was a good time to practice moving things around his room with his mind, or to read with a flashlight under the blanket, or just to think about everything that was happening to him.

Days after school he waved goodbye to the other kids and would race home to squeeze down to finger size and explore the garden or play with the squirrel that had saved him from the cat. The squirrel would let Christopher, holding tightly to the fur around its neck, ride on its back. They went so high and fast through the branches of the big elm tree in the backyard that Christopher thought his chest would burst.

The squirrel didn't trust him when he was full size until one day, when Christopher put half of a shelled walnut on the bricks of the patio a few yards away from his feet. It took about five minutes for the squirrel to spot it from a high branch in the elm and come down after it. But just as the squirrel was about to pick it up with its paws,

Christopher shifted it with his mind, at first to one side and then to the other, but always a little closer, until the squirrel, getting mad, jumped on his knee instead and took the other half of the walnut right out of his palm and ate it sitting there.

From then on they were friends, though Christopher often wondered what the squirrel thought about its strange new playmate who was sometimes as small as a leaf, and sometimes as big as a small tree.

People seemed different somehow. He noticed it first in the way his mother kept asking him if he felt all right. Was he sick? Was he in trouble at school? She seemed so worried all the time that he finally decided *she* was having trouble in her office, and when he asked her about it her face and neck turned bright red and she never asked him again—though he did catch her staring at him once in a while.

He was getting the same kind of treatment from his friends. They acted as if they were walking on eggshells around him, especially after the day he stopped Johnny Dawes from beating up on little Frank Hopje. Christopher didn't particularly like Frankie, but the two boys were making too much noise during recess and frightening the baby birds nesting in the big oak tree that grew in the corner of the schoolyard. With all the shouting going on, the birds were nervous and wouldn't let Christopher touch their feathers with his mind so he told Johnny to leave Frankie alone. Johnny was furious at being interrupted and turned, ready to swing at Christopher; but after one look at his eyes Johnny just shrugged and walked away.

And the girls treated him differently, too. Their eyes were soft and round when he caught them looking at him, and they immediately looked aside when they saw him catching their stares.

Most of all, though, he noticed the difference in his teachers. He had Mrs. Stout for arithmetic as well as homeroom, and she must have been taking lessons herself because she was really getting good at explaining things like long division and fractions. In fact, one Friday during recess she showed him some short cuts that allowed

[63]

him to do an entire week's homework assignments in less than twenty minutes.

That same day Mr. Fried assigned the English class a really neat book to read and report on. It was written by a man named Salinger, and Christopher got so interested in the kid in the story that his book report was five pages long—two pages longer than the assigned length.

So in spite of a run of beautiful spring days he was sorry when school was out and it was time to go home. He was also sorry when the afternoon ended and Frances called him in to dinner. And he was sorry when he got so tired that he finally fell asleep in bed at night. There were just too many great things to do to waste time sleeping.

The days ran swiftly by until one afternoon he found himself in front of the old house on Sheridan Road and realized he hadn't been to the Headmaster's for almost two weeks! He pulled the rusty chain and worried if he had missed any lessons. The door opened at once. For a moment they just stood there, looking at each other, saying nothing. Then the Headmaster smiled and nodded.

"Come in." He turned and led the way to the office. He sat in the chair behind the desk with the blue folder in front of him. "You look as if you've been having some fun."

Christopher started to nod and then quickly said, "Yes, sir." He felt calm and excited at the same time, like when you're about to see *Star Wars* for the third time.

"From here on things will begin to look a little different to you," the Headmaster said.

"Yes, sir. They already do."

"Oh? Hmmmmm." The Headmaster looked up sharply and tilted his head. "Yes. I see." He opened the blue folder and paged through it and then wrote a short note with his pen.

"Good. Then that problem will take care of itself." He paused for a moment and then continued. "I think you're ready to hear this now." He closed the blue folder and looked at it thoughtfully. "Most of the time when people don't get along with their friends or family it's because they're not getting along with themselves. If you don't like yourself, how can you expect anyone else to like you? And if you don't think people like you, it's easy to be careless about their possessions or about their feelings. Next thing you know they *really* don't like you, which only convinces you that you were right in the first place. See how it is?"

"It just goes round and round, feeding on itself," Christopher said.

"It's what they call a self-fulfilling prophecy, and the only way to stop it is to change the basic cause—which is to start liking yourself. That breaks the spiral and starts a new pattern. You like yourself and expect others to like you, too. You care about them and they show that they care about you, so you like yourself even more.

"Like most things in the world it takes only a tiny, tiny change at the right place and time to make a really big change somewhere else. The problem is, it isn't always easy to know where the hinge pin is. Do you know what I mean?"

Christopher said, "Yes, that little rod in the middle of the hinge that the door swings on."

"Right. It isn't always easy to find the hinge pin, but once you do you can really change the world around you. Learning how to use your ESP powers is that kind of hinge pin in your life, and now that it is started it will be fairly easy to expand on it. We'll let you exercise your muscles a little more in this next lesson before we move on to the next level. Okay, lecture's over. Let's go to the 'jump' labyrinth."

Headmaster put the blue folder into the drawer as he always did and then led the way out of the library and up the stairs to the second floor. He opened a door to a large, airy room. Except for a small space near the door, the entire floor was covered with a platform divided into dozens of box-like compartments with sides

[65]

about six inches high. The compartments had no tops and some had small openings cut into the sides like tiny doors between adjacent compartments. Each compartment was painted a different color and several had small objects in them—Christopher could see a marble, a jack, some coins, and a gold ring.

Headmaster sat on the edge of the platform and put the gold ring beside him. He said, "You'll practice this at small size because you will find it a little easier and, of course, it saves space. First, sit up here beside me and let's go small." And before Christopher could even get his head in order, the Headmaster disappeared!

He looked around frantically and then down at the platform and sure enough, there was the Headmaster no bigger than his thumb looking up at Christopher impatiently with his fists on his hips. Quickly Christopher took control and within a few seconds he was the same size.

Headmaster walked over a few steps and picked up the gold ring. It now seemed about the size of a pie plate. "Take this. It will help you get started. Let's go in here."

He led the way through a doorway cut into the wall of a compartment on the platform. The walls were painted a gold color, very similar to that of the ring Christopher held, and in one wall there was another doorway to a neighboring compartment that was painted a bright red.

"Hold the ring in front of your face and look through the hole into the next room. Now I want you to imagine yourself diving through the ring and landing in the red room. Don't close your eyes. Okay? Go."

Christopher knew he had to reach into himself for the power, and then with a quick thrust he just sort of pushed through the ring and suddenly he was there! He turned quickly and looked back through the doorway. The Headmaster was standing there looking at him with a wide grin and, even as he watched, the Headmaster disappeared from the other room and was standing beside him.

[66]

"Very good. You got that faster than anyone I've ever taught before. Have you been practicing a lot?"

Christopher nodded, his eyes still wide.

"Okay, I want you to try eight or ten 'jumps' using the ring. At first you'll just point it at a doorway and 'jump,' but then try it right through a wall. If you look carefully through the ring, you'll see the color of the next room which will give you something to aim for. Go ahead now, and I'll catch up with you later." The Headmaster walked back through the doorway to the gold room and disappeared.

Christopher "jumped" from red to green to pale blue and then to a room painted a deep blue-black. He soon became familiar with the sense of gathering himself together and mentally thrusting himself through the ring. He found he could control how far into the next room he would "jump" and in the end, by looking extra deeply, as if through a ring within the ring, he could see the color of the room *beyond* the next room. He made "jumps" where he skipped one room and then two. Pretty soon he had only to think of the color and with a quick glance through the ring he found himself there.

And just as the power to move small objects with his mind made him acutely sensitive to the things in the space around him, Christopher discovered that the power to "jump" gave him a strong sense of the rooms and where they were in relationship to each other. He could have drawn a map of the whole labyrinth just by extending his senses out from his body. He was listening in all directions when he struck a place of such enormous power that he recoiled quickly.

"Sorry, Christopher. I didn't know you were 'reaching.'" It was the Headmaster talking to his mind! "Okay. Now try some 'jumps' without the ring, and when you have the hang of it give me another call."

It was almost too easy. The first couple of times Christopher needed to imagine that the ring was still in front of his face, but soon he could call up the thrusting sensation without any picture of the ring in his mind. And it was easy to do the next task when the Headmaster asked him to "jump" coins and marbles from room to room by themselves.

He stopped finally, a little tired, but feeling wonderful about the lesson. He "jumped" to the gold room and then walked out and expanded to full size sitting on the edge of the platform. In a moment the Headmaster was sitting beside him.

"Here's talisman 101," the Headmaster said. "You'll find it's a lot harder to 'jump' when you're full size, and I want you to develop both distance and control during the next week. Take your time and get good at it because we have some tough ones coming up."

The chime sounded softly in the background. "There's the bell," Headmaster said. He looked full in the face at Christopher for a moment. "I'm very pleased with you, Christopher."

Christopher practically floated home, he was feeling so good about himself and about the whole, wonderful world. He ran the last three blocks and leaped up the back stairs two at a time hoping to beat Crackers to the door and surprise him. But the house was quiet when he slammed through the back door and he skidded to a halt in the middle of the kitchen. Frances was sitting at the table, her hands in her lap, and Penny was there, too. Neither of them said anything, they just sat and stared.

Christopher couldn't think what he had done this time. "What's the matter?"

Penny screwed up her face and started to cry. "It's Crackers," she said. "He's gone!"

"Gone? What do you mean gone?"

"Gone. Disappeared. Run away!" She started to wail.

"I let him out back after his dinner as I always do," Frances said. "And he never came back. Penny and I both have been up and down the whole neighborhood, and he's just not anywhere!"

Christopher looked at them, not knowing what to say. Crackers wouldn't run away, they all knew that. Crackers loved him, loved

[69]

them all. What could have happened? Was it possible that someone had stolen his dog? Crackers was so friendly he'd follow anyone who petted him or played with him, but he knew when Christopher would be coming home. In all the five years of his life, Crackers had never missed meeting Christopher when he came home for dinner.

Not thinking clearly, Christopher turned and ran out the door. He raced up the back alley shouting, "Crackers!" and then with his special whistle, "CRACKERS!" He ran over to the lake where slippery, moss-covered rocks leaned over the deep water.

"CRACKERS!" he shouted as loudly as he could, remembering how the dog struggled in the water when his coat was wet and heavy and the waves swept over his narrow nose. If Crackers had chased a gull, or even a dragonfly, which he liked to do sometimes, and had slipped on the rocks, he might be drowned!

But there was no sign of him in the water. Perhaps he went up to the university campus with some kids playing Frisbee. Christopher started running along the shoreline, stopping when his side hurt too much, shouting and whistling all the way. It was taking too long and he was tiring too fast. He needed to "jump" the way he had been doing in Headmaster's maze. But first he had to catch his breath. He could feel himself breathing too quickly. It was making him dizzy.

He stopped and tried to calm his pounding heart. He tried to control the breath that caught his throat. He tried to straighten up against the sharp pain in his side. Still gasping a little he reached into his pocket and took out the talisman that had "101" engraved in its side. He quickly held it between his fingers and squeezed hard.

He wanted to "jump" to the big field in front of the campus where the students play Frisbee football. It will still more than ten blocks from where he was, but that was no farther than the "jumps" between rooms in the labyrinth.

He looked straight out to where he wanted to go and willed himself there.

Nothing happened.

He looked again, then closed his eyes and reached deeply into his worried brain.

Nothing. He was rooted to the spot like a bush or a tree. He could feel the distraction and worry splintering his concentration and strength. He'd never be able to "jump" this way and find Crackers. He started to run again, but now his side began hurting at once and it doubled him over in pain. He limped along as fast as he could, thinking, where is the Headmaster and his power when I really need him? What is the use of all the practicing and work if it can't even help me find my dog?

"CRACKERS!" he shouted as loudly as he could. "Come on, boy."

He put two fingers in his mouth and blew. But his mouth was too dry. He couldn't even whistle.

And when he got to the field there was no one playing there at all. At the far end two students lay against a tree, reading books; otherwise the field was completely empty. Crackers wasn't there.

Christopher dropped to the grass and started to cry. The tears just pumped out of his eyes and dripped down his cheeks. He remembered Crackers' beautiful red coat and the way he pushed his nose into Christopher's hand when he wanted to be petted, how his ears flopped when he raced to meet him after school, and the way he leaped at his face licking his ears and cheeks and neck. A world without Crackers would be the most dismal, miserable, lonely place he could ever imagine.

There had to be a way to find him. Christoper took out the talisman and looked at it. "Help me, Headmaster," he shouted silently. "Help me, please."

He let the quiet of the field enter into him. A light breeze ruffled the surface of the grass, and he let the sense of his body and the grass and the air and the light just grow and expand like a great reaching out of his arms. He let his reach spread and spread out to the edges of the field, and then along the paths and the buildings of the

campus. Then he reached out into the streets, the houses, the stores, and offices. Out, farther out, to the high school across town, and south past the railway station. He could feel the whirlpools of energy from groups of people in the supermarket, from the automobile engines, and a great pulsing pressure from the power station.

He closed his eyes now and looked within the vast space for Crackers, for his dog, his friend; and suddenly he thought he got a faint scent, a flavor, an impression so light and delicate he couldn't look at it or think about it without scaring it away. Open and receptive, Christopher just let the sensations flow in. Yes, there was something there. A sense of pain and blackness. He faced in that direction and imagined a gold ring in front of his closed eyes. He reached through the ring with all his strength and immediately felt the jolt that told him he had "jumped."

He opened his eyes. He stood in a bare hallway. The floor was covered with worn linoleum, the walls were painted an ugly green. There was a smell of medicine in the air. It had to be a hospital of some kind, but not as large or organized as hospitals usually are.

Christopher heard dim voices coming through a closed door. Quietly he pushed the door open and looked around it. Two men were standing with their backs to him looking down at something on the table. A bright light hung over their heads. There were metal cabinets around the sides of the room and a rolling cart with a white towel and metal instruments just to the left of the door.

He moved into the room fearing what he would see on the table, yet knowing already what was there. Both men had turned when they heard the door, and between them he could see Crackers' rust-red coat. He was lying on his side, not moving. A clutch of fear grabbed Christopher's chest, and squeezed. He moved forward slowly, staring. Crackers just lay there, not moving, maybe not breathing. A small moan came out of Christopher's throat.

The man in a white doctor's jacket was tall and heavy. He had a lot of gray hair sticking out around a bald spot in the middle of his head. His face was patient and kind. "Is he your dog?" he said.

[73]

The other man was smaller, but still a head taller than Christopher. He wore a checkered shirt, and his face was sunbrowned and leathery as if he worked outside a lot.

Christopher nodded and moved between them, reaching out to touch Crackers' head.

"Careful," the man in the white coat said. "He may have a concussion."

"He just ran across the alley in front of the truck," the other man said. "I barely touched him. It wasn't my fault." There was a whiny note in the voice that Christopher didn't like.

Just then Crackers sniffed loudly and his tongue came out and licked his nose. His eyes opened and he tried to lift his head, but it was obvious he had trouble focusing. His foreleg jerked as if starting to scratch, but the eyes clouded and he let his head lie back on the table.

"There are no bruises or broken bones," the doctor said. "He hit his head on the pavement and was knocked out. He may have a mild concussion, but it doesn't look serious." He leaned down and gently slid Crackers' eyelid up to look at the eyes. He pointed a small flashlight at the open eye.

Crackers lifted his head again and sniffed at Christopher. He made a small sound in his throat and reached up as if to lick Christopher's face. But he couldn't move that far, so he settled for Christopher's hand and then just rested his chin on Christopher's arm.

Christopher hugged him to his chest and rocked slowly. Crackers was going to be all right. He knew it. But it was no thanks to the driver who must have been driving too fast down the alley. Crackers never ran across a street without looking, but he thought the alley was just part of the backyard and he never looked. It had never mattered before. Cars rarely used the alley except to go to their garages, and trucks came only to make deliveries of some kind. The speed limit was supposed to be five miles an hour. At that speed Crackers could have run between a truck's wheels and still been safe.

[74]

Christopher felt the anger blow up inside of him. "You were driving too fast! What were you doing in the alley anyway? You could have killed my dog! You nearly killed Crackers!"

He looked up at the man's face and saw the weakness and guilt in the pale eyes which shifted between Christopher and the doctor.

"He just jumped in front of my wheels," the man's voice began to rise. "You're supposed to keep a dog like that chained up. He's not supposed to be running around free on the streets!" He backed away from the fury in Christopher's eyes.

All the agony of the last hour built up into a knot in Christopher's chest. He reached out with his mind for anything loose in the area and got ready to hit the man with bottles and pans, with the books on the shelves, and the steel tools that lined the tray. He saw a pair of pointed scissors and a row of sharp scalpels on the cart. It would be easy to plunge them into the man's chest. The fury and hatred seemed to flow up through Christopher's body and out through his hands which clutched Crackers stiffly. The dog moaned deep in his throat and then twisted and tried to stand in Christopher's unyielding arms.

It took only a second for the realization to hit him. The man wasn't worth it. He was weak and foolish, but he hadn't hit Crackers on purpose. Christopher's powers were too important to be wasted on him.

With Crackers licking his neck he felt the tension flow out of him. Almost absently, he patted Crackers' head and scratched behind the ears. The tail waved wildly and Crackers' paws began a quick, slipping scrabble on the slick metal surface of the table. Christopher looked at the man's face, his weak eyes and chin, the stooping shoulders.

"You could have killed my dog," he said quietly. "Or you could have hit some kid." And then he just looked straight into the man's eyes, not saying anything else for a long, long time. He watched the man's face change. It strengthened, and the eyes steadied. He lifted his head and pulled his shoulders back.

[75]

"I brought him here as quick as I could," he said in a kind of apology. "I hope he'll be all right."

The doctor nodded. "Looks like he's okay. Call me if he stumbles or walks funny."

Crackers jumped to the floor and started cruising the room for the way out.

It was a long walk back home, but Christopher refused the offer of a ride. Crackers stayed close by his side and sat patiently at his heels when they waited for the red light to change on Main Street.

That was the first time in his life Christopher had felt stronger and more powerful than an adult. It was a strange sensation, and he wanted to get his head all the way around it before he forgot. Up to now, whenever he'd challenged an adult it was by lying or pretending. This time he'd stood right up to the man and stared him straight in the eye. He hadn't used any of his powers and he didn't feel now as if he wanted to get even. They were quits.

There were all sorts of things about it that Christopher needed to think through. By talking quietly and seriously he had made the man listen and understand, which he probably never would have done if Christopher had lost his temper. They had each kept their self-respect—if anything, the man had been sure enough of himself to apologize and accept fault without blaming Christopher or Crackers. There were other things to think about, too: how just *feeling* strong made you strong, even if you didn't flex your muscles or hit someone.

He wasn't even close to being finished with his thoughts by the time they got home. Frances and Penny and his mom and dad all crowded around, fussing at him and at Crackers—glad to see they were both all right, gasping when he told them about the truck and the vet's office.

"I don't think that man will be speeding down alleys ever again," Christopher said, remembering the look on the man's face as he and Crackers had walked away from the vet's front door.

All right, let's get on with it. I'm not sure how it will work out today. This is usually a tough lesson.

Headmaster led Christopher out of his office and to the very end of the hall where a narrow staircase ran down to the basement.

"This is an anechoic chamber," Headmaster said as he opened a door. "What we do is eliminate all distracting sensory information so that you can concentrate."

He flipped a switch which turned on a dim light in one corner. In the middle of the room stood a large tank looking like an oversized bathtub. About a foot of very clear blue water lay flat as glass in the bottom of the tub. The tub stood on an open screen of metal wires which was suspended several feet above the floor of the room. He and the Headmaster also stood on this metal screen. Walls, ceiling, and the floor below were studded with large pointed cones of black foamed plastic.

The sound of the Headmaster's voice in the room was curiously muted and small. "There will be no light, no sound, and as little feeling as it is possible to give you. When I leave, you will take off your clothes and lie in that tub. The water is at exactly 98.6 degrees

Fahrenheit—the same temperature as your blood. It is also saturated with salt so that you will float high in it. Don't worry about falling asleep or turning over. You cannot possibly sink, and it is very shallow.

"When you get in, just lie quietly. You may put your hands behind your neck to support your head if it is more comfortable that way, but that is more necessary for adults than children of your proportions and weight. Then just open your mind and listen. Think about the feeling you have when you are moving objects with your mind.

"If you become frightened, I'll help; but there's nothing to be frightened about."

Without another word the Headmaster turned and went out, closing the door quietly behind him. When it was closed Christopher could not find it again. The black cones merged from ceiling to wall to floor in an unbroken pattern. Slowly and reluctantly he slipped out of his shoes, socks, shirt and pants. The air was warm and the water even warmer, so he dropped his shorts and stepped into the tub. Just as he lay back in the water and felt it support him, the light went out leaving the room pitch black and absolutely silent.

He heard his breath going in and out of his lungs in a deep, heavy sigh. It sounded like a monster movie on television. Then he heard his heart beating, thump a-thump, thump a-thump. For a long time he listened to the workings of his body. He heard a high-pitched hissing in his ears which worried him at first, and then he decided it must be the blood circulating to keep his head working all right.

Then he forgot the sounds and watched the blobs of color flashing across in front of his eyes. He knew them from before. He had often seen them at night with his eyes closed. They were blue, mostly, and outlined in a glowing white and they bounced and squeezed in weird shapes.

Pretty soon they faded and he found himself just staring and listening. With his mental fingers he explored the walls of the room, the softness of the foam, the silky wetness of the saltwater. He floated quite still and seemed not to be moving, until his little toe touched the wall of the tub and with the gentlest of pushes sent him back to the center to lie as if in a great black cloud.

Through all this he was dimly aware of a kind of music playing in the back of his head. He often heard music that way—as if a pair of stereo speakers were mounted at the two back corners of his brain— but he had never heard this melody before. It was a thin, sad sound, very faint when he paid attention to it, but clear and firm when he was thinking about something else. Now, as he sort of gentled it—not looking right at it, so to speak, but encouraging it with a friendly feeling—it grew louder. The single tone was joined by another and the two musical voices played in and out of each other, first separately, and then together in a wonderfully harmonious duet. Then a third voice joined in, and this one had a familiar timbre to it. It was music, but it was words, too. A soft murmur at first, but then he could feel words spoken musically like the quicksilver flash of a fish in the watery depths of a flowing stream.

And now, of course, Christopher knew the voice and understood the words. It was the Headmaster sending him images of a great city. Tall, graceful buildings seemed to rise out of clouds. They were linked with lacy bridges that went from spire to spire. Strange aircraft slipped through the air without wings or helicopter blades to hold them up. A reddish sun shone high in the sky but gave little warmth or light. The walls of the buildings seemed to give off their own glowing light. He felt the Headmaster urge him on, and together they floated through the air of the city. Strangely, there were no people in the buildings or in the flying machines. Christopher knew it without being told. The city was dead, or nearly so, even though it looked as clean and bustling as a brand new supermarket.

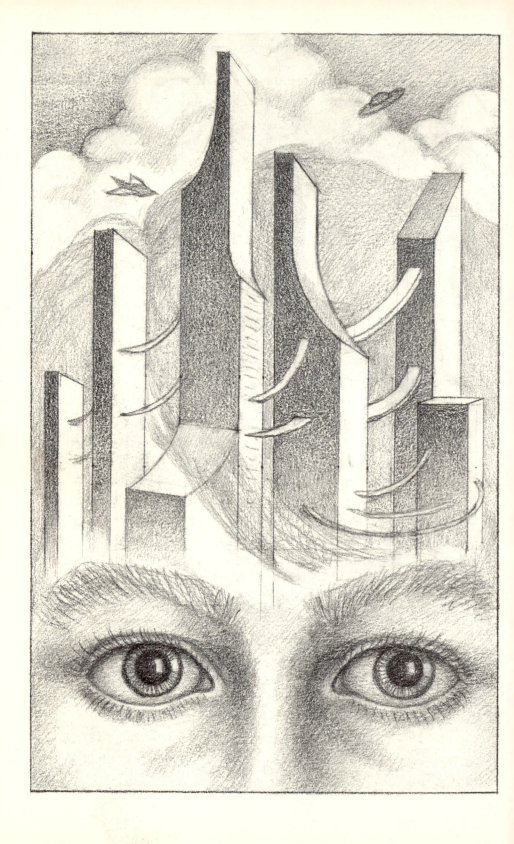

Then the city disappeared and he was back in the black room. Headmaster's voice was still with him, flashing him pictures that had no words, of an old and wise people who were tired and had reached some kind of ending. It wasn't clear how it was to end, but Christopher sensed the sadness of a good time past and the quiet eagerness to get to where they were going. They felt a responsibility to pass on what they had learned and so had devoted a segment of time—and Christopher knew it was a very long time by his standards—to give others their power and insight.

"Do you understand, Christopher? Do you hear me?"

Christopher nodded and then sent his own mental acknowledgment. He had many questions still, but he had too much to think about to know what to ask just yet.

Quickly he rose out of the tank. He had no need of the light to find his clothes and to dress. His skin was dry even before he started to pull on his shirt. The door opened in front of him and he went up the stairs and back along the hall to the Headmaster's office. Without a word he took the talisman marked "110" from the Headmaster and then, in a gesture he was never completely to understand, he reached up and touched the Headmaster's cheek. He left with a quick wave of his hand and was back in his kitchen and phoning his mother minutes later.

Yes, he was home, he told her. He was about to go out again. No, he wouldn't stay out after dark though he would like to see the sunset before coming in for dinner. His mother didn't know what to say. Watching sunsets was hardly a regular pastime for the Christopher she knew.

On the beach an hour later he saw a cherry-red sun sink into a maroon puddle far, far out in the lake. It was a magic time of day. He liked the way people tended to walk alone, most of them deep in some sort of conversation with themselves. Some of the weirder types talked out loud, but even the silent ones had their eyes in that flat, empty stare that meant they weren't looking at you at all. It

[81]

gave Christopher a sense of privacy and aloneness that he liked. He sat on the beach sand with his arms around his knees and was able to look straight at the last sliver of sun which suddenly winked out. It would be dark quickly now, and he wanted to get as much as he could out of the twilight before heading home. He slipped the talisman out of his pocket and squeezed it.

Almost at once he began to hear the people around him. A girl, sitting against the fence with a book on her knees, was broadcasting a string of words. She was totally absorbed in the book and all he got from her was what she was reading. As he extended his "reach" he picked up a man walking on the grass behind the beach. This was much more complicated. He had words intermixed with pictures and underlying all a current of powerful anger and fear. It was like a rollercoaster ride with signs and scenes flashing by too quickly to examine closely.

Christopher got dizzy at the crazy speed of it all and had to pull back to find his own center. He limited his attention to the sand between his shoes, his fingers, the tear in the cuff of his pants, which reduced the chatter to a soft background murmur in his head. Now, more cautiously, he probed outward and started receiving the stream of words again from the girl.

The book was a reading assignment for a course she was taking. The language was English, but old and difficult for her. Christopher could not understand the words, but he could see the images the words were making in her head—an old dirt road, a horse-drawn coach bouncing and uncomfortable for the passengers, a woman dressed in layers of silk, a man in knee breeches. Darkness and rain outside. He could also feel her reactions—boredom with the story and a wish to get it all read, vague stirrings of hunger, a face of a girl friend, the feel of a boy's sweaty hand in hers. She looked up and Christopher was suddenly seeing the beach, the water, a dark shape near the water where someone was sitting hunched over. With a start he realized he was looking at his own back. She decided it was too dark to read anymore so she just kept looking around. He could feel her liking the quiet loneliness of the moment, and then a quick chill went through her body and she decided to go home.

It wasn't anything at all like the time he had been in the dark room, listening to the Headmaster. That had been crisp and clear, with sharp outlines to the thoughts and to the words. With the girl, and even more with the man who had walked by, the messages were blurred, words mixed with images and feelings. They made him dizzy. He was going to have to be very careful when he reached out or he'd get physically sick from the impact of other people's minds.

The girl left, and Christopher, too, felt the chill and decided he'd better head home. As he approached the back door he reached out with his mind again and was almost bowled over by Crackers' excitement. The dog had run down from the upstairs bedroom and was jumping and barking at the kitchen door, panting and eager to welcome Christopher home.

When he opened the back door, Christopher was overwhelmed. He had never known an emotion so powerful as the rush of love he felt coming from the dog. The images were colorless and blurry, but the scents of the kitchen, the back porch, his own body, were stronger and clearer than he could ever imagine a smell to be. He hugged the dog and felt Crackers' delight in the thin arms around his body, the delicious salt taste of boy-sweat on his long, flapping tongue. Christopher was able to calm the dog by just standing quietly and rubbing his ears. He withdrew his attention from the dog, then, and reached out into the rest of the house. Frances was in the kitchen, Penny upstairs doing schoolwork. Frances was thinking about the salad greens in the bowl in front of her. He could feel her hands cutting the vegetables and at the same time hear the song that was repeating in her head. Suddenly she became aware of his watching her from the back door. He could feel her little start of surprise and then the complex wash of feelings she had about him.

He stared at her, confused. After the unmixed simplicity of

[83]

Crackers' love, Frances was almost more than he could take. He felt her anger and irritation at the way he made extra work for her—she was mad because she had had to mop the kitchen floor that morning and it wasn't mopping day. He had spilled a glass of juice. She was mad at finding an old doughnut on a shelf of his closet. Yet there was a sweet-sour flavor in her mind as she looked at his bright eyes and skinny body and he felt her want to hug and protect him, cuddle him in her arms.

"Your dinner's just about ready, Christopher. Get washed and tell Penny. I'm just leaving."

Christopher just stood there staring at her until he felt her beginning to wonder what was wrong. Then he nodded and started upstairs. He brushed her arm gently as he passed close to her.

In the bathroom he wet his hands and wiped the dirt off on the towel, then ran down the hall to Penny's room and stuck his head in the door.

"Dinner's ready," he said.

Penny turned from her desk and sent him such a blast of anger that he nearly fell. He thought he heard her scream but her face was calm. "All right. I've just got to finish this page. You start, and I'll be right down."

He backed away, puzzled. How could she be so calm outside and so furious inside? And anyway, what was she so mad about? He went downstairs but kept his mind up in her room. Penny turned back to the desk and tried to remember the end of the sentence she was writing. It was a story for her English class and the ideas had flowed nice and easy onto the page until that brat Christopher had to come to interrupt.

Then the words came back and quickly she wrote them out. She added her name to the top of the sheet and folded it carefully into her notebook so that she wouldn't forget it in the rush to get dressed and out the next morning.

She headed downstairs thinking about the kid. (With a start, Christopher realized she meant *him*.) He had been acting strangely for days now, maybe weeks. He wasn't after her all the time, teasing or nagging. He seemed to be taken up with something of his own. She wondered if he had a girl friend.

Maybe he was finally beginning to grow up and out of his craziness. She thought about inviting her friends over for a pajama party and again could feel how much it hurt when they wouldn't come the last time. Christopher felt that same blast of anger from her, but this time he wasn't so surprised. With some effort he pretended not to know what she was feeling as she came into the kitchen.

They were still eating dinner when he became aware of his mother striding up the street. She took a train to work every day and when the weather was nice she liked the walk home from the station, but tonight she was tired and still thinking about a problem she was having with someone in her office.

As she saw the house her thoughts shifted forward to getting out of her office clothes and into a hot bath. Christopher had stopped eating and was just staring at his fork as he followed her up the path, through the front door and now entering the kitchen. He didn't look up as she paused in the doorway until he felt her concern.

"Hi," she said. "Christopher? Are you all right?"

Christopher turned to face her but almost dropped his fork when he felt the full force of her thoughts about him. Her love was a warm, physical, touching thing that had memories of him small and hugging close in her arms, of him crying with a jagged cut in his finger, of a heart-squeezing moment of fear when he had jumped off the garage roof and into an enormous pile of snow in their backyard.

Yet under the love he sensed a current of despair and worry that was always with her. She was never sure that he would be home when he was supposed to be, that he would not have fallen into the

lake or out of a tree, that he hadn't got into a fistfight or talked back
to a teacher, that Frances wouldn't quit because he had tramped
mud across her kitchen floor once too often, or left his room in such
a mess it would take two extra hours to get it cleaned.

Most shocking of all was what he felt under the despair, and when
he understood what it was he looked up at her with such amazement
that he was certain *she* could read *his* thoughts. For a long moment
they stayed looking at each other without speaking.

She was *afraid*. Afraid *for* him and what he might do to the
outside world, which would make the outside world hit back at him
without mercy.

But what had Christopher staring at her, was that she was afraid
of him as well—of what he might do to her if he lost his temper and
of what he might do outside that she would feel responsible for. He
had never thought of it that way. When *he* got into trouble she felt it
was in some way her fault, too! She had to apologize to the parents
of the kids he got into fights with. She had to replace the books he
borrowed from the library and lost. She had to make it up to the
world and then apply some sort of punishment to him, and she was
never sure he would take the punishment and not run away.

In that long moment of understanding he felt so sorry for her he
thought his heart would break. He got up from the table and walked
toward her and put his head on her shoulder without speaking. She
dropped her purse on the counter and held him, her fingers moving
gently in his hair.

"Hey, what's this?" she said softly. He sensed the worry explod-
ing through her so he stepped back quickly.

"Nothing's wrong, Mom." he said. "I just saw how tired you
looked so I figured to give you a pick-me-up hug."

She looked at him a little suspiciously. "Penny?"

But Penny just shrugged. "It's a new phase, I think. He's pretending to be human, but I don't think he'll fool anybody."

[86]

"How would you know anything about being human?" Christopher shot back at her.

His mother sighed loudly. "Okay. Cut the chatter. I'm heading for the tub. Please pick up after you get done down here; I don't want to have to clean the kitchen before starting dinner for your dad and me."

Penny had finished eating and was putting her dishes in the dishwasher while he sat watching. It had never occurred to him for a second that any adult would be afraid of him. He was just a kid in a world run by, owned by, controlled by grown-ups. Anytime he stepped out of line she could send him to his room, ground him, even spank him. She had all the marbles; why should his mother be frightened of him? The more he thought about it, the less he liked what he had seen in her mind.

Penny looked at him curiously. "What's happening, Chris? Are you in some kind of trouble?" He read the real concern in her and shook his head quickly.

"No. I'm okay. It's just that, well, everything seems different somehow. Listen, you can invite your friends to stay over if you want to. I won't bother you."

Penny stared at him. "Christopher. You can be so nice sometimes," she shrugged her shoulders helplessly, and he heard her finish the thought in her head but not say it, "—but how can I be sure you'll keep your promise?"

"Try me. I mean it," he said.

Her face wrinkled as if she were going to cry and without a word she turned and ran up to her room.

Christopher was rinsing off his dishes and putting them away when he heard the garage door open, and in a few seconds his father came in through the back door. He was thinking about having to repaint the steps when he saw Christopher at the sink.

Again Christopher was hit by a wave of thought, this time from his father, that had him gripping the sponge tightly and squeezing his eyes together in surprise and pain. He had been thinking about this moment all evening. They didn't spend a lot of time together, but in almost every way he could think of, his father was the most important person in his life.

His mother was warmth and love and the place to go when he was hurt. With her he was reassured that he was a real person and worth something.

His father was where he went when he needed to understand something about himself or about the world. It could be as simple as fixing his bicycle or adding fractions, it could be as complicated as whether there really was a God. His father would then stop whatever he was doing and talk—not telling him that this was the way it was and the only way, but always as if to say, this is the way it looks to me and you might think differently about it. He would show Christopher how fractions were like pieces of a pie, or how a bicycle chain was pushed around by the gears, and with his deft hands would find and straighten the bent metal making it look so easy and simple you could feel dumb for having to ask.

And lately, when the questions had become more complicated, his father usually started off by saying, "Some people believe . . . " It was very annoying because Christopher just wanted the same simple answers he'd always got. But it was more interesting, too.

Christopher knew how impatient his father could get, and knew his anger. The anger was like a blast of heat that could singe your eyebrows and burn your face. It was like a volcano that exploded with fire and poured molten rock in all directions, only the fire and heat were words that would stab straight into your chest and smolder there for days.

He stood at the sink and cautiously opened his mental ears to hear his father's thoughts. The flavor was crisp and clear—not as controlled as the Headmaster's, but having that same orderly feeling. There was a start of surprise and pleasure at seeing Christopher washing his dishes. And then came the moment Christopher was never to forget for the rest of his life.

It was the one thing he had never expected. He looked for the right word and then suddenly found it. His father *respected* him. He thought Christopher was bright, smart, sensitive to what was happening around him, perceptive, all kinds of good things.

Christopher found he was holding his breath as he let the feelings wash over him. He also sensed the undercurrent of concern—that Christopher didn't think well enough of himself which made him angry and inconsiderate; that it was so difficult to make him see that the way he treated others had so much to do with the way he was treated in return; that until Christopher could get inside the feelings of other people he might never learn to get along with them.

Oh, Dad, Christopher thought, if you only knew.

He turned away from the sink. "Hi," he said.

"Hi. Your mom home yet?"

Christopher nodded. "Taking a bath." He didn't trust himself to say any more.

Without taking his eyes away from Christopher's, his father put his leather case on the table. They just looked at each other.

"Your mother is worried about you. She thinks something is going on that you're not telling us. You want to talk about it?"

Yeah, Christopher thought, I'd like to talk about it with you, Dad. But I can't.

"It's okay," was all he said. "You don't have to worry."

His father put some ice in a glass and filled it with orange juice from the container in the refrigerator. He loosened his tie and sat down at the table.

"I hated being thirteen years old." he said. He took off his glasses and started rubbing his face and eyes. "Do you hate being thirteen?"

Christopher didn't know how to answer. "It's okay, I guess." He could hear his father trying to think of a way to say what he felt. It was amazing. He really cared.

[89]

The silence between them lengthened, but it wasn't uncomfortable.

"We haven't played chess in a while," his father said. "Want to play a game later?"

Christopher laughed to himself. His father wouldn't have a chance against him now! "Sure, Dad," he said as calmly as he could. "I'll even make a bet on it if you want. Double or nothing on my allowance. What do you say?"

His father must have had some mind-reading power too. "No, not your whole allowance, but I'll bet you an ice cream sundae against a car wash. How's that?"

"It's a bet!" Christopher said.

And, of course, he beat his father twice, hardly trying.

It took some effort to turn off his mental "ears" that night, but when he did he fell asleep at once—deep, dreamless, absolutely blacked-out sleep all night long. It had been the longest and most surprising day of his life.

For days afterward he continued to be surprised by what people had in their heads. The first thing he noticed was that grown-ups' faces mask what they're thinking. His teachers could be standing in front of their classes, stonefaced, waiting for a kid to answer a question, when inside they were thinking about lunch, or a book they were reading, or how their feet hurt. Once when Johnny Dawes made a pretty raw comment about Mrs. Stout's legs, Christopher heard her laughing to herself and thinking her new stockings were great at the same time that she made Johnny stand outside in the hall for the rest of the class period.

But it was sad sometimes to feel a teacher's frustration when a class was noisy and acting up. You just couldn't keep a joke going at someone's expense when you knew how that person was feeling inside, so more and more Christopher found himself a quiet by-stander or actually breaking up the kids' fights or noise, whether it was in the classroom or out in the schoolyard. Johnny got fed up with him at one point and shouted, "What's the matter with you these days? You trying to be the teacher's pet or something? Come off it, Chrissie-baby, or I'll meet you after school and teach you some manners."

So Christopher waited until the final bell and took Johnny to the empty lot down the block where a half dozen of their friends watched as he put four careful punches into Johnny's stomach (where they wouldn't hurt Christopher's knuckles) and then slapped him, openhanded, right off his feet. Johnny never laid a hand on him.

When Johnny got his breath back Christopher took him home and gave him a couple of Frances' chocolate chip cookies. He felt badly about the red fingermarks he had left on Johnny's left cheek, but liked very much the respect he read in Johnny's mind.

Most people, he discovered, were fuzzy thinkers, and it was hard to understand them. When he walked down the street or through a crowded supermarket he learned to keep the listening door in his mind almost completely closed, otherwise the noise would have made him crazy. But occasionally he would hear a clear, strong voice, and when he did he always made a special effort to get close to the person and perhaps even speak to him or to her.

The first was a lady pushing a shopping cart who was practicing her part in a choral group. She sang her part and heard the others as well and he could even see the signals from the conductor. But as soon as she approached the shelves her thoughts shifted to her shopping and she jangled unpleasantly.

The second was a boy who couldn't have been much more than six or seven who was carefully whittling on a stick. His concentration was so clear and hard that Christopher could actually see each wood fiber as it came under the knife edge.

The third was Headmaster sending a clear call for his next lesson and Christopher thought, of course! That's how he did it all the time! And so with a big smile on his face he presented himself at the old house after school and was met with a thin answering grin from the Headmaster.

Christopher followed him into the library and took one of the leather chairs in front of the desk. Headmaster picked up the blue folder, skimmed through it quickly—there were many more pages in it now than when he had first seen it—and then dropped it on the desk and joined Christopher in the other chair in front of the desk. He leaned back for a moment with his fingers making a steeple in front of his lips.

"I've been with you from time to time over the last week so I know what's been happening. We could spend the rest of our lives talking about how different people think and feel, but what I want to hear is how it seems to you, and what you think is the most important thing you have learned from being able to listen in on others' thoughts."

Christopher hesitated. That was a big question. "Well, two things, really. First, I discovered that people aren't as mean inside as they look on the outside. Why should that be? It's true of kids just as much as it is true of grown-ups. Mostly they're afraid, and the more afraid they are, the meaner some people look."

"Think about yourself," the Headmaster said. "Didn't you do the same thing? Act toughest when you were most scared?"

"I guess so." Christopher knew it was true. "I just never thought that other people would feel the same way that I did."

"What was the second thing?"

Christopher looked away. "It's kind of embarrassing."

The Headmaster waited quietly.

"It's just that, except for Penny, people don't hate me as much as I expected."

"You could put that in a more positive way, couldn't you?" Headmaster didn't smile.

"You mean . . . everyone seems to like me more than I thought they did?" Christopher had trouble saying it out loud.

"Right. Now, what about Penny?"

[93]

"She really hates me sometimes." Christopher felt a rush of hurt and anger and he couldn't say any more.

"Yes. We don't have time to go into that right now, but in time you'll discover why. And I think you'll also find that sometimes hate is very close to love—as if they were on the opposite sides of a coin—and that it is easy to hate the most somebody you love a lot, or once loved a lot.

"But those are two very useful discoveries, aren't they? That people are nicer inside than they look on the outside, and that they generally seem to like each other—even a troublemaker like you." He softened the words with a small smile.

He went on, "What do you think might happen if everyone in the world could read minds now the way you can?"

It was a startling idea.

"Well, no one could get away with lying of course, because you'd know, wouldn't you? And you'd know right away when someone liked you, or didn't like you. Of course, there might be a lot of bloody noses around at first, but mostly I think people would be surprised to find out that their enemies weren't enemies at all. I guess people would pretty soon find out who they wanted to be with and who they didn't."

"And in general," Headmaster said, "People might get along better with each other. In fact there wouldn't be much need for wars if people understood what others wanted, or needed, or how they felt about things."

He stood up and sat on the edge of his desk. "It would be very good for the human race if people could all hear each other's thoughts the way you can, Christopher, but unfortunately they can't. You remember way back when you first started with me I mentioned your PQ? That's the *psi* quotient which has to do with your psychic abilities. It has to be well above 150 on the scale we use for you to learn what you have to.

"The average for untrained humans is about 50, which is far too low for them to pick up each other's thoughts. The natural score of very young babies is around 100, but they get so much pressure from their parents or other people nearby that they quickly close the door on their powers. They have to protect themselves from all that noise, right?"

Christopher nodded. "Yes, sir. But it's easy to stop the noise once you know how."

"Yes. But little babies don't have that control yet. They just know they're being bombarded, so they close the door and never learn how to open it again. The power is locked up for good and, for the most part, they get along all right. The trouble is that it's getting so crowded in this world that if something isn't done soon you'll have a nuclear war and that will be the end," he said.

Christopher felt a chill go up his back. He'd heard his parents talking this way and read it in the paper now and then, but never really believed it could happen, at least not until years and years in the future.

"So what we're going to do—you, and a few others like you—is teach people how to open their psychic doors a crack, at least enough so that they can hear each other dimly, if not completely. Let's go over to the lab and I'll show you what I mean."

Headmaster led the way to the room next door where Christopher first learned how to roll the steel ball on the glass table. Headmaster had him sit in the soft leather chair again and lean back with his eyes closed while he went to the instrument bench and flipped a couple of switches.

"I'll do it this time. Just listen and watch." The words were crisp and clear in his mind. At first they hung in the dark, empty spaces of his brain like a deep, echoing voice. Then they faded and were replaced by a face—it was Penny, looking off into the distance in a pensive way. Christopher knew at once that she was in the school library, and he could hear the drift of her thoughts as she tried to concentrate on her reading assignment but kept being interrupted by thoughts of an argument she had had with one of her teachers.

Christopher felt the tug of the Headmaster's mind and followed as he brushed past her surface thoughts and down into the depths of Penny's thoughts and feelings. It was as if they were descending into the basement of a big house. At the foot of the stairs they had to take a careful detour around a vortex of spinning wind that gave off a high-pitched whistle, and then past an enormous frame full of shifting color and shape. Christopher watched it, fascinated, for a long moment, but the Headmaster beckoned him on. A great engine was throbbing rhythmically in a room of its own, and as they passed the doorway Christopher could feel the heat coming from it.

They moved through rooms of old toys and furniture—a broken doll, a crib, a worn pink blanket—and then the Headmaster stopped. They stood in front of a closed door. It was locked and tightly barred from the outside, and the surface was covered with a thin layer of dust and grime.

Headmaster was like a glowing light chasing the shadows away. He reached forward with a sort of warmth and, where he touched, the dust melted away. The door swung open before them and Christopher followed the Headmaster inside. A baby wrapped in soft blankets lay sleeping in the small, windowless room. Headmaster leaned forward and touched the child's forehead. Christopher could feel the message of warmth and safety coming from it. The baby opened its eyes. The Headmaster nodded and then beckoned with his head for Christopher to follow him. They left the room with the door open a crack and in a moment were back in the laboratory.

Christopher opened his eyes and watched as the Headmaster flipped off a few switches and then returned to sit in the chair opposite.

"I use the equipment as an amplifier to help us work over longer distances. When you do it by yourself, you'll find it only possible if you're fairly close to the person.

[96]

"Now I have to caution you. You're going into people's very private places. You don't want to disturb anything and if possible they shouldn't ever know that you were there. Don't touch anything but the door, and then waken the child if it is asleep. It will almost always be a child. It will almost always be a locked room. If it is not, you'll have either to get out and leave it alone, or else deal with whatever you face.

"Time is curious in this work. You'll find almost no real time has passed—the clock will register a difference of only a couple of minutes, though it may seem like hours to you.

"And all you want to do is awaken the child and leave the door open so that it can hear what is going on outside and come out when it grows strong enough.

"Do you have any questions?"

Christopher was still breathless with the wonder of Penny's mind. The power and color were so rich he felt he could have spent the rest of his life exploring that wonderful place.

"Is my mind like that?"

"You can look and see for yourself, can't you?" The Headmaster smiled. "Try it, you may like it."

They went back to the Headmaster's office, and he pulled open the wooden cabinet and took out the talisman marked "111."

"Here you are. You'll need this the first time or two."

He made a final note in the blue folder and then seemed to sign it with a flourish. He closed the cover and then leaned forward over the desk.

"I'm sorry to have rushed you, but I had very limited time. You have done well, Christopher. Don't expect enormous changes in Penny, or the others, right away. They need to build some strength and confidence in their abilities, and that will take awhile."

Christopher was very quiet. He could feel the anticipation growing inside him. He was about to start the most exciting adventure of his life, and best of all he would be doing it on his own and using what he had learned to be good at.

[97]

Headmaster held open the door to his office as Christopher nodded and went out, still lost in thought. As he closed the front door behind him, he thought he heard the chime faintly in the background announcing the end of the hour.

That evening at dinner he kept watching Penny curiously until she finally said, "What are you looking at?" and he had to stop.

Still, she wasn't as angry as usual—he could feel it—and when she left to go up to her room he said, "Goodnight, Penny."

And she said "'Night, Chris," in a soft voice.

Two days passed before he felt the situation was right to try it on his own. He and Johnny Dawes had been doing laps around the track, and in a final burst Johnny had done the last straightaway at top speed so he was well ahead when they passed the finish line. They both flopped down on the grass, their chests heaving, and as they got their breath they lay quietly chewing the tender white ends of pulled grass.

Christopher could feel Johnny's openness so he slipped the talisman out of his pocket, squeezed it, and began to reach into Johnny's mind.

It was a little like Penny's—a big house with many rooms. Some were open and obviously used, but a little sloppy, with newspapers and magazines lying around, and discarded clothes. He saw a baseball glove and bat, old tennis shoes, torn school books. Some of the doors were partially blocked so you couldn't see inside. Others opened to empty rooms.

Christopher moved carefully to the back of the house and then downstairs. Here things were more interesting. A big machine of some kind, like a power generator, was running in one corner, and in another stood a monstrous fan, like the propeller of an old airplane, creating a strong breeze.

Down one more level, and Christopher knew he was getting close. Here old toys lay scattered about—a sled, a pair of worn ice skates, a stuffed dog with one floppy ear torn off. The locked door was low and small and blended so well with the wall that Christopher nearly missed it. He reached out to touch it and felt the strength flow through him and to the door which opened inward.

Christopher bent down and went inside. It was a very tiny baby—perhaps too small to live, Christopher thought—and when he touched its face it opened its eyes for just a flash but went immediately back to sleep. Perhaps Johnny had been locked up too soon, he thought, as he withdrew.

He left Johnny's mind quickly and then just lay beside him on the grass, listening. After a few minutes he stood up, but Johnny didn't get up too. "You go on," Johnny said. "I think I'll stick around here awhile." He lay back with his head on his hands, the weed sticking up from his mouth at a jaunty angle.

Christopher said, "Okay," but he was disappointed. He felt he had failed somehow. He headed up toward the university campus reaching forward with his mind. He walked slowly, testing the minds that he passed on the street, but he was reluctant to enter the private worlds of people he didn't like, when suddenly he was struck by an absolute explosion of sound and light. It was music, like a huge pipe organ echoing from the rafters of the biggest church in the world. It was like being in the center of a fourth of July rocket sweeping up into the sky and then bursting open in an expanding circle of fiery light.

He pulled back quickly and then probed more cautiously. Could he try it here, right now, in the street like this? It was a young woman, he could feel it, and she had the richest mind he had ever known. Every corner was filled with wonderful things—rugs and paintings, poetry and music, sculpture and words echoing down long halls. He passed a room with a group of actors reading a play, and in another the space was filled with glowing lines that made incredibly beautiful geometric figures and shapes in space.

One room frightened him. The door was open, but inside it was black with a blackness that absorbed light, so that he couldn't see an inch beyond the threshold. And when he reached forward, his hand just disappeared in the darkness! He withdrew quickly and went downstairs. It was clean and dry, and when he found the door he was looking for he was amazed to discover it was already partly open, but jammed against a brick. He pushed the brick aside and went in.

The child sat looking at him with enormous eyes. It was a girl of perhaps eight or nine, and she came forward at once and stood in the doorway looking out. Then she turned and said, "Thank you."

For a long time they stood staring at each other. Then, without a word, Christopher withdrew and found himself on the street again. He looked around curiously. There were few cars and no people. On his right a row of tall bushes hid a home, and as he approached the walk he saw a woman sitting on a porch swing.

"Who is it?" she called out.

"It's me—Christopher," he said.

He walked toward her and then stopped, uncertain. There was something strange about the way she held her head and stared out at the bushes.

"Come closer; you don't have to be afraid."

Still she was looking past him, and suddenly he realized: the woman was blind! He let his mind reach out for her and knew that she could feel it.

"Hello," she thought with a little surprise in her tone. "Who *are* you?"

Christopher didn't know how to answer.

"Just a kid. I live near here," he said. He could feel her curling to the touch of his mind.

"Oh, how nice that is," she said.

Christopher sat on the porch railing beside the lady for a long time that afternoon. They didn't talk much, they just sort of explored each other with mental fingers. Her blindness had made her mind far richer and more colorful than any he had seen so far. It was as if she had compensated for the blackness outside with all the color and sound she could imagine. And by letting her look into his mind she could know for the first time what it was like to walk down a street with tall trees on either side, to watch a dog run with speed and grace, to see a table set and ready for dinner. Her wonder became his, too, and he was grateful to her for showing him how marvelous it was to be able to see. Finally he knew that she was tired and a little sad, so he said goodbye and headed home.

Penny was there, and Crackers, and Frances all sitting in the kitchen. They had been talking about him. He could feel it in the mental echoes in the room and by their quick silence when he walked in. He didn't care. The radio was playing a bouncy song, and he felt so good that he pulled Frances to her feet and started to dance around the kitchen with her.

"You see," she said to Penny, "he's crazy!" And they all laughed as she sat down huffing.

It was fun, and easy to be silly with people you liked and you knew liked you. It was as if he could take risks or act or look dumb and never worry that they'd stop liking him or think he *was* dumb just because he acted that way sometimes. And suddenly he understood something his father had been telling him for years and that had never made sense before.

"You aren't what you do, anymore than you are what you write, or a test you fail, or a room you leave in a mess," his father used to say. "So when your mother or I scold you it's because we are objecting to your *behavior*, not objecting to who you *are*, or loving you any less."

The new understanding and, even more important, belief in himself, wiped away a fear he had had of his father ever since he could remember. His father was big and strong and stern-faced, and when he was on your side the whole world could come after you and you'd be safe. And now Christopher knew his dad would always be on his side, no matter what he did.

It was a lot less scary, then, to do what he knew he had been avoiding. The next night his father and mother were in the family room watching the late news when Christopher came in and sat on the floor beside them. He had squeezed the talisman with "111" engraved in its side and felt very strong, but still a little nervous as he reached out into his father's mind.

Right from the beginning he knew he had to be very careful. It was not a very big house, but the rooms were all clean and attractive. The furnishings were carefully placed and well used, and there seemed to be books on shelves everywhere. Many were like the large bound volumes he had seen in his father's office. Oddly enough each room had a scale, a big old chemist's balance in one room, a small spring scale in another, a steelyard in the third.

As he made his way through the house, he had the curious sensation that the house knew he was there and was watching him. He moved down a long hall looking into the rooms as he passed. Near the end of the hall he noticed a closed door, and he thought he could hear murmurs and his mother's soft laugh. He didn't look inside.

Downstairs a big furnace put out a lot of heat, and a circulating pump chugged away. The flue needed a coat of paint and some of the valves looked old-fashioned, though still serviceable.

He looked around and then felt an ominous silence. For a long moment he waited and then, without time to think, dropped to his knees as a winged creature of some kind went whistling past right where his head had just been. And from a side passage he heard a whisper of sound as a heavy hammer came flying through the air, again right where he had been standing.

Suddenly very frightened, he called out, "It's okay, Dad. It's me, Christopher."

He could feel the shock that went through the entire house when he shouted. A mattress stored against the wall just lifted itself up and started moving toward him, crowding him into a corner.

"Dad! It's me," he shouted again, but the mattress had reached

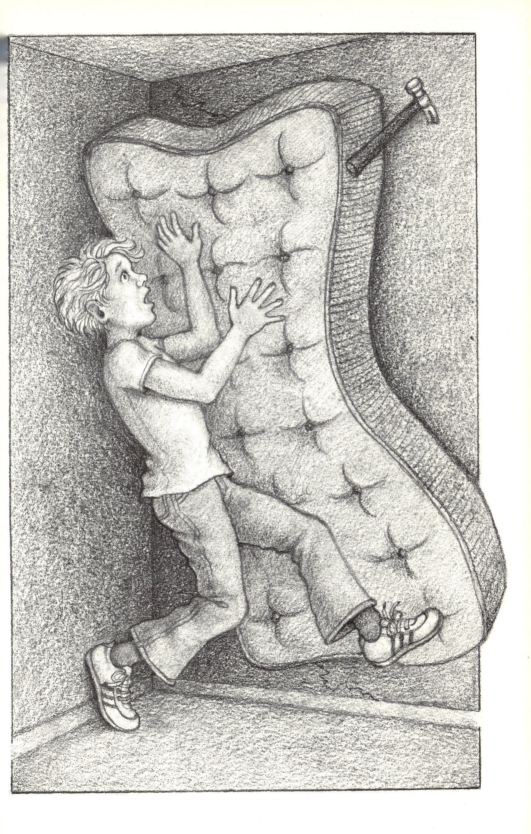

him now and started pushing heavily against him, trapping and squeezing him against the wall.

"Dad!" he gasped. Held like this he couldn't move forward or backward. He couldn't get out!

Heart pounding, breath short, he began to fight back. He let his mental muscles swell and slowly he built up pressure until he could breathe again. Then quickly he stepped around the mattress, which rolled into a tight cylinder on itself squeezing the space where he had been. Again the flying thing went past overhead, but this time Christopher reached out and touched it and at once it disappeared. Now reaching into himself again for strength he let a calming light flow out and around.

He found the locked door in a corner of the cellar. The lock was old brass, but well oiled, and the door was a beautiful carved wood. It was clean and it opened at a touch. Christopher stood in the doorway, amazed at what he saw. The room was dimly lit by a small lamp that stood on a desk in its center. A young man sat reading and making notes with a pen.

He looked up at Christopher. "Sorry about the mattress. Reflexes are much faster than reason, aren't they?" Then curiously, "How did you get in here, anyway?"

Christopher told him about Headmaster and the old house, about the polka dots and the cat in the backyard, about the kid nearly getting killed under the wheels of the car. It didn't take any time at all. He just sort of sent it in a quick flash, and the young man took it all in just as fast.

The man smiled. "I don't get out much any more but if you're going to be rattling around out there I might be tempted. I'm very proud that it's you, Christopher," and he came out from behind the desk. Christopher ran to him and held him tightly around the waist. The young man hugged him close and then rocked him gently. It was wonderful not to be alone anymore.

A burst of warmth and light flowed over him, and Christopher opened his eyes. His mother had just turned off the television set. "I'm for bed," she said.

Christopher and his father looked at each other for a long moment and then his father said, "Me too, dear. Goodnight, Christopher. Sleep well."

Christopher walked down the shady street toward the old house feeling as if he owned the whole world. He knew the Headmaster would be pleased with him. After the evening with his father he had put the talisman with "111" engraved on its side in the drawer with the others. There were seven of them now, all the same size and shape, but each with special feelings more memorable than a book of old photographs.

Since the evening with his father he had become a lot more skillful and at the same time more selective about the minds he went into. It wasn't that it was dangerous—no one was ever again going to be able to trap him the way his father had—only that some people just weren't ready to be opened up, and he got so he could tell the difference just by "tasting" their surface thoughts for a few seconds.

He reached forward for the Headmaster but, as usual, got no response. The Headmaster was the only person he knew who had the ability to set up a total block. Still Christopher was looking forward to seeing the thin little man with the hatchet face and deep-set eyes. He paused at the gate and looked at the house. It was amazing how old and decrepit it appeared on the outside and how clean and functional it was inside.

In late summer now the path was almost completely choked with weeds, and dead vines hung unkempt and ragged from the walls and the porch roof. The smell of damp mildew was strong near the front door, but the wooden handle still hung from its rusty chain.

Christopher pulled at the handle, disappointed that the Headmaster hadn't sensed his presence and come to the door already.

He waited what seemed like a long time, and when there was no answer he pulled the chain again. The paint had long since blistered on the front door, and it was peeling in ugly strips showing the cracked and raw wood of the door. Christopher noticed the door was not tightly shut. Perhaps the Headmaster had left it that way for him, expecting him just to come in as usual.

Hesitantly, he pushed at the door which seemed to move on stubborn hinges. He stopped and stared. It wasn't the Headmaster's house at all! The first thing he noticed was that the air was filled with dust. Dust covered the floor and walls. Cobwebs and spiderwebs filled every corner and clung to the old newspapers that littered the floor. Christopher walked into the front hall, his mind in shocked surprise. A few broken sticks of furniture lay about, and in the living room a ratty old couch stood tilted on three legs, stuffing and springs showing.

A mouse went scuffling into a corner, frightening Christopher for a second. He stepped carefully over a bookcase that lay across the doorway to the dining room.

It was entirely different from what he remembered—not just the dirt and mess, but the shapes of the rooms, the doorways, the windows.

Christopher reached out with all his power, listening, sensing, *feeling* the spaces around him, looking for some hint of where the Headmaster had gone.

[107]

But there was nothing. Just an old, abandoned house filled with ghosts, maybe, and memories.

He turned and walked out, closing the front door carefully behind him. He knew where he had to look for the Headmaster now. There was only one place left on earth where he was going to be but he would be there for as long as Christopher lived.

"Try it," the Headmaster had said about looking into his own mind. "You may like it."

And Christopher knew he would always find the Headmaster there.

A single tear insisted on running down his cheek as he headed home.